MOONDANCE

URBAN FANTASY & PULP HORROR CAST IN NOIR

J. D. BRINK

FUGITIVE FICTION

CONTENTS

MOONDANCE

YOUR FREE BOOK

The infamous Eight-Ball Gang has returned and they're blazing a path of mayhem across the Midwest. Silk Spider is the super-powered femme fatale assigned to bring them down.

Behind the Eight-Ball is a story of noir superhero action, dark humor, and wild entertainment set in the celebrated superhero realm of the Identity Crisis Universe.

Get a FREE download of this noir-styled tale of capes and crime by going to:
https://BookHip.com/PVKZMK

MOONDANCE

URBAN FANTASY & PULP HORROR CAST
IN NOIR

EATING IN THE UNDERWORLD

It takes a bastard to find a bastard. And I've found plenty.

Toys help: bugs with filament transmitters in their wings, cyberspace robins following binary breadcrumbs, but these can only get you so far. A real detective's feet are flatter than his ass, and his eyes are as cold as his heart. You want to do the job right, you have to walk the trail yourself, go look the suspect in the face and see if he blinks.

That's what I've come for today, though I don't tell Gene's secretary that.

She gets a more polite version: that I've come to see the big man himself, good old Gene Sizemore, the one the Libra Foundations bigwigs just can't stop talking about.

She smiles and politely invites me to have a seat.

Vel is the girl's name—it says so on the neon-blue nameplate of her translucent plastic desk. She's got long slim legs, dark hair, a nice chest, full lips. She's damn near perfect. So naturally I figure her for a doll.

That's Gene's business, after all.

I sit on a gaudy purple couch and pretend to appreciate the erotic crystal sculpture screwing itself on the coffee table. The waiting room is small with yellow walls to contrast the purple furniture.

Gene's never had very good taste.

There are three vidscreens mounted in a column up one wall, one on top of the next. The top and bottom screens are smaller and showing a gravball game and stock market scores, respectively. On the big central screen is a vid made to look like paparazzi footage: some bald-headed corporate-type pushing his way through a crowd of admirers, a sexy woman on his arm and a broad-shouldered bodyguard at his back.

It's a doll ad running in twenty second loops.

Attention spans these days.

I watch it more than a dozen times, then clear my throat, check my old-fashioned pocket watch, and give Vel a smile.

"It should be just a few more minutes," she says, pleasantly smiling back. Her lipstick's lavender, like her dress, like this factory-dead cow I'm sitting on.

I let the ad roll nine more times, then stand up and remove my trench coat. I work a finger in behind the knot of my skinny black tie and drop my fedora on a purple chair.

But any impression of impatience is wasted on Vel, as is my classic private dick look. It's custom fashion these days, but worth the price. Style's important if you want to be professional yet intimidating. And I do.

"You think he's doing any work in there?" I ask.

She gives a polite chuckle. If she is a doll, she's at least been given a sense of humor.

Not that I was joking.

I've been watching Gene's work habits. He never puts any effort in past 3:30, and it's 4:33 now.

Just like in college.

Gene was one of those brainiacs that could screw off and still get the grades.

One more reason I never liked him.

Another was that he somehow managed to get nice looking girls. Take the pink-haired number I saw down stairs. I watched her elevator stop at this floor, Gene's floor, before I came up.

She's in there now.

She's what he's doing.

The intercom lights up her plastic prism of a desk like a back alley emerald.

"Mr. Celeste," says Vel in her angelic voice. "Mr. Size-more will see you now."

"Thank you, dear."

I collect my coat and hat and go on in.

The walls of the inner office are veneered in polished black glass. There's a real leather couch set before a large two-piece desk made to look like slabs of granite. The pink-haired girl I saw downstairs is on the couch. She could be Vel's twin, but for the hair. She's wiping her mouth with the back of her hand while Gene's standing with his back to me, pulling up the zipper on his metal-lic-green suit.

The girl looks first, flashing her bright blue eyes at me.

I admit, I'm frozen there for just half a second.

Then Gene turns and shoots his big mouth at me, ruining it.

"Hey, Harry! Long time, no see!" His hand jams into mine, grip soft, like his belly. Old Gene's put on a few pounds, and lost some of those blond locks he used to sculpt just so.

"Sit down, sit down," he says. "Seph, slide over."

The pink-haired girl scoots her skinny ass to one side and I sit.

She smells good, like a woman.

"Seph?" I ask. "Like short for 'Seraph'?"

"*Ha!* Hear that, baby? Harry thinks you're an angel! No, it's short for Persephone."

He takes his seat, a BodCradle 1200X, its spidery legs crouching between the two slabs of plastic granite. The chair alone speaks of his success. *The throne of any office kingdom*, the ad says, fingertip interface with all your office goodies while molding to and massaging your ass.

All the chair doesn't do is blow you, which Gene seems to have covered.

He gives me his damn salesman's smile. Some things never change.

"So, Harry, what are you up to these days? Still working for the company? Sorry I've never come by to visit."

"No, I don't," I tell him. "And don't worry about it, we've both had busy lives. Didn't exactly part as the best of friends, either."

He shrugs at me, bygones being bygones and all that.

"Besides," I say, "when I was working for Libra full-time it was across town at the Pyramid. Wouldn't expect to see you over that way."

"The Pyramid, huh?"

He's jealous. Gene works for a satellite division of Libra Foundations called BioFacture. He's not big enough to get into the Pyramid.

I play it modest for him though: "Don't worry, I only had a third-floor cube. Just a resource tracker, not an executive-type, like you."

Resource tracker is polite corporate jargon for *fraud investigator*. Gene pales a little and his BodCradle sputters under his nervous squirm.

"Out on my own now, though."

"Freelancing, eh?" There he finds something to bolster his confidence again. "I always wondered what that liberal arts degree would get you, Harry!" He laughs it up.

Twentieth century film, actually, but I don't bother correcting him. I just smile and flatter: "We couldn't all be scientific geniuses, buddy boy. Here, I brought something for you."

I reach into my trench coat and pull out a gun.

He gets to his feet pretty damn quick.

The girl beside me takes a sharp breath.

"Whoa." My turn to chuckle. "Wrong pocket."

Though I know damn well which pocket is which.

"You carry a gun?" he squeaks.

"Sometimes, but this isn't a *real* gun. It's a spacer, a stun gun." I put the weapon away, flip my folded coat over, and produce a fifth of vodka.

"Rasputin Number Five," Gene says, sitting back down. "That's good stuff."

He fingers a button on his fancy chair and a tray of crystal tumblers rises from one slab of desk.

I glance at the girl next to me. She's eyeballing me with those beautiful blues, licks her lips, but not seductively, not for me. More like a starved animal.

Seph wears a moody blue dress, spaghetti strapped, no makeup. Her pink hair is short but wild.

He and I get three fingers of liquor. The girl gets nothing.

I inquire, but Gene says, "Nah, she doesn't drink—not that anyway," then laughs that annoying damn noise of his.

I steer the conversation toward college stories for a while, giving him time to loosen up on my laced vodka. Magenta Nail relaxes a target five times faster than drinking alone. My liver plugs filter it out.

At one point a story heads dangerously close to Gigi, but I manage to dodge her, reminding him instead of a party the campus cops had to break up.

Gigi was Gene's best girl, a little French number who ended up in my bed on more than one occasion. I still say I did him a favor, that she'd have just broken his fragile little heart, but Gene never saw it as a heroic act on my part.

No, this topic would ruin the drunken camaraderie we're building and likely derail everything I'm working toward.

I take another sip and am suddenly aware of the body heat next to me. Seph feels closer, but I dare not look, not with the threat of Gigi just a story behind. Still, I can't help but wonder what kind of a furnace the doll's got, and what kind of heat it can kick out.

Eventually, after a few more laughs and another glass, I let him get back around to asking me why I'm here.

"Were you just feeling nostalgic," he asks, "or were you thinking about getting a doll?"

I shrug.

His glazed eyes narrow, all sly.

He fingers his chair. One shiny black panel on the wall lights up.

A girl, Vel and Seph's triplet sister, appears on screen, this one a red-head in a naughty little schoolgirl uniform.

"No, wait, wait," he slurs. "You're in the private investigator business. Maybe you need a partner?"

The wall screen changes. There's a thick-necked man in a yellow suit, dark skin, shaved head, shades.

"The Aegis Crown 4-Charlie," he says. "Bodyguard model. Best thing about a doll bodyguard, they don't mind taking a bullet for the boss, you know?

"Or maybe you want someone more subtle? Someone that blends into the underbelly crowd?"

The screen blinks to a muscled white guy with a goatee.

"Aegis Crown 5-Alpha. The Bravo model is coming out soon with hidden weapons built into its hands. Slightly different look, too. Police buy these to do undercover work, or blend into the background on raids, then pop out on their side. Big contract.

"Best part is," more annoying laughter, "we need to keep making new ones so the bad guys won't recognize them, you know? So soon there'll be AC 6's. Going to look Asian."

"I didn't realize the doll biz was so big."

"Oh, yeah, buddy. Bank. *Bank!*"

He takes another big swallow, then spins away for a refill.

I feel a warm touch on my leg. The girl's hand is there, then gone.

Gene turns back around, the cup at his lips.

"I've already started laying designs for our next big hit: the Venus and Adonis lines. Hollywood's been clamoring for us to make doubles of actors and actresses, for stunts and such, you know? But the Actors' Guild is fighting it. The big stars don't want to be replaceable. Then anyone would be able to make a Stone Wagenborg movie, you know?"

I'd heard of doll doubles being made for foreign officials, to act as bullet magnets for assassins and attend meetings while the diplomat is off screwing someone other than his wife, things like that. But those aren't the dolls I'm interested in today.

"What about her?" I ask, nudging the girl next to me. I feel those blue eyes on the side of my face again.

Gene's big mouth spreads into a sloppy grin. "Our most popular model. The Velvet Rose."

The naughty schoolgirl returns on the wall screen.

"The latest version available is 6-Delta, like Vel out in the lobby there. I sell four or five a month! Bank, buddy, *bank!*"

The pink-haired girl gets up and walks around to the back of the couch, out of sight.

"And this one, here?" I say. "She's a Velvet Rose 6-Delta?"

Gene starts laughing, then shushes loudly—himself or me, I can't tell. He sets his tumbler of vodka on the desk, leans down toward me.

"Buddy..." His hand is on my knee now. "Let me let you in on a little secret."

He looks behind me and motions to her.

Persephone struts out from behind me, her perfectly tailored ass twitching like a cat in heat. He leans back to let her sit on his lap. The chair whirs in stereo as it adjusts to the new weight.

"My sweetheart, here, she's unique."

His hand strokes her leg.

The girl doesn't seem to notice; her eyes are on me.

"Harry, you're looking at the only Velvet Rose 6-Echo in existence. Made her special, just for me."

That's what I've been waiting for: Gene's drunken confession to his old college chum.

I take another sip of vodka, looking at her over the rim of my glass. "What makes her so special," I ask, "besides the obvious?"

"Well, you knew I was a genius, old buddy, but not like this...

"I redesigned her nutrition-impulse system, see. Most dolls eat baby food and have a natural hunger for it, meets all the nutritional requirements for their pseudo-parts. Persephone here, though..."

Big shit-eating grin.

"Her brain has two items on its menu, but she'll always prefer filet mignon over hamburger, caviar over crawfish.

"And what, you may ask, is this delectable, gourmet must-have dish? Are you ready for this?

"*Semen!* Male seed, my friend!

"And being the charitable guy that I am, I keep her from starving, if you know what I mean!"

More laughing. Hungry-hyena laughing. I-screwed-the-girl-and-the-company-and-I'm-getting-away-with-it laughing.

That's why I'm here.

His hands rub either side of Seph's ass, rocking her back and forth on his lap.

She just stares at me.

I try not to feel sorry for her. That's *not* why I'm here.

So I play out the rest of the scene, tell him he's a goddamn Leonardo da Vinci, congratulate him on reinventing Eve and all that.

"Have to meet with a client across the street," I say. "Just thought I'd stop and see old Gene on the way."

I polish off what's in my glass, set it on the couch, and toss my business card next to it. "Keep in touch, buddy-boy."

I hear lips smacking and the metallic rip of his zipper on my way out the door.

Good old Gene.

Still an asshole.

THE NEXT MORNING I'm in my office, a rented space in a cube building. Mine is one of twenty on this floor alone, a modest room dressed to my tastes: a desk of real oak, fake leather couch, freestanding coat rack, antique Bogart movie poster. I have a small desktop interface, not much compared to what I had at the Pyramid, but I prefer it that way.

I like a modest operation.

Libra Foundations eliminated my job and the whole in-house fraud department in the cutbacks of '42.

Best thing that ever happened to me. Freed me up to follow my own vision, even if I do miss the regular paycheck bit.

And hell, I still get Libra money—they're one of my best clients.

Now that my suspect has been confirmed, I easily trace the money trail back to Gene.

I could see before that resources had been redirected from various departments over to the BioFacture side of the Libra house. Digital dough stashed in secret hiding places or run down the back alleys of cyberspace. Now I can pick up at the final destination and work backwards, linking up to those tracks I'd lost before.

I do have to give old Gene credit: he's a smart guy. He managed to steal funds from fourteen different places, relatively small amounts that wouldn't leave big gaping holes for the accounting boys to notice. At least not right away.

But his homemade girlfriend cost the company a quarter-mill, and when the quarterly report hit the accounting chief's desk, she saw the big picture.

That's when they called me.

***

There's a knock at my door.

I hit a button and the whole front wall shifts from an opaque off-white to one-way transparent.

Seph stands on the other side, clad in a red leather vest and matching mini-skirt, pink hair in spikes.

I open the door, see no sign of Gene in the grid of hallway, then invite her inside.

She slides between me and the door jamb, rubbing against me, her deep blue gaze driving through my dull browns.

My eyes slip downward.

Her vest is zipped low and she's wearing nothing under it. The skirt is cut high, the cleft of her ass peeking out.

"What is this?" I ask, sealing the door. "Is this Gene's attempt at a bribe?"

"He doesn't know I'm here," she says. Her voice has the same pitch as Vel's but the tone is different, less confident.

"I didn't know you could talk," I say. "You didn't say a word yesterday."

"He doesn't like me to talk."

"Not what he made you for, eh?"

She shakes her head. Her eyes are naive but hungry.

I take my fedora from the rack and set it on my head —an attempt to stay professional—then sit on the corner of my desk.

"Well, if he didn't send you, how did you find me?"

"You left this for me." In her hand is my business card. "'Harold Celeste, investigations.'"

"Harry," I tell her.

"Harry."

We stare for a moment in silence.

Her eyes go to the floor. She inches up to me, rests her head on my shoulder, snuggles in close.

I resist, arms at my sides, hands gripping tight on the desk edge.

"I didn't really leave that card for you," I tell her ear. "It's a business card. It's what people do."

"What else do people do?" she asks. Her voice is innocent, the question child-like. It occurs to me that she really doesn't know.

My hands wrap around her slender shoulders and I kiss those full, ruby lips. It's like kissing Gigi, young and inexperienced. But Seph catches on quickly.

While we're tongue wrestling, she works my pants open. Then she's feeding.

I can't bring myself to stop her.

When she's done, I gently push her toward the couch.

Getting her naked is easy; there are only two articles to free her from. But she looks a little confused.

"What are you doing?" she asks.

I realize that this is the point that Gene's always done with her. He probably goes back to work or watching the game, sending her off to some corner to sit while he drinks a beer and pats himself on the back some more.

"Showing you what else people do."

She helps me out of my clothes.

It's like teenager sex the first time, awkward and exploratory.

The second is better.

———

AFTERWARD WE REST on the couch together, her on top of me, a layer of sweat between us.

Her breathing is soft, regular. I wonder if it's her heartbeat I feel or my own. I'm not even sure if she has a heart, but she's certainly more human than I imagined.

"What are you?" I whisper.

I feel her warm breath on my chest: "Persephone."

"Do you know the story of Persephone?" I ask, twisting out the spikes of her pink hair.

"In the days of Greek mythology, when the gods were still as complex and relatable as people, there was this girl named Persephone. She was the daughter of Demeter, goddess of the harvest, which made her a lovely little thing.

"And beautiful young girls always attract attention, especially from all the bitter old men who never had any when they were young and life was still good.

"So lovely little Seph caught the smoldering, blood-shot eye of Hades, god of the Underworld. See, there wasn't much in the gloom down there to look at, woman-wise. That's how it is when you have a job nobody wants and live life in the back-alleys of Hell. So he took a fancy to her and set a trap.

"One day, when Persephone was out for a long walk alone, she came across this beautiful black rose rising up out of the middle of the road. When she bent over to smell it—*boom*—the earth cracked open and belched fire and brimstone and out popped Hades in all his terrible glory, riding his dark chariot with black horses pounding the dirt and snorting fire. And he grabbed her and stole her off to the land of the dead to be his bride."

Persephone looks up with concern.

I smile and continue.

"So while her daughter was down there, missing from all the world, Demeter went frantic. She was looking high and low, never eating, never resting, wearing herself pretty thin.

"And being as she's the goddess of the harvest and vegetation and all, the earth got to be worn out too: greens turned brown, birds stopped singing, and the weather went cold.

"Finally she went up to Olympus and begged Zeus, who could give a shit what happened as long as he had a fresh mortal girl every once in a while to screw in animal form.

"I guess old Zeus was into bestiality or something.

"But anyway, Big Z saw the whole thing from way up on Olympus and knew his brother Hades had Seph down lighting up his miserable life in the Underworld.

"So Demeter headed south—I'm talking *way* south— and found Seph down there having a tea party trying to cheer up dead people and such, and finally convinced old Hades to let the girl go home.

"But by then it was a little too late.

"Persephone was down there a long time by now, and after she'd gotten over being afraid of everything and got a little more comfortable, she'd finally accepted her husband's offer to have a snack. She ate just one pomegranate seed—being a skinny young thing she was always on a hunger strike so she'd look her best—but that one seed was enough.

"Once you eat in the Underworld, you're stuck to it.

"She was allowed to go back to the surface with her mother, but every year, Seph had to return and spend time with her husband, like it or not. And while she was gone the earth would wither and go cold, missing her so much.

"And that's how the Greeks said winter came on and later greened back into spring."

We lie here a minute more, quiet breathing and cooling in our sweat.

Finally Seph says, "I don't want to go back."

"You have to," I tell her, then add: "For a few more days, anyway."

"Then what happens?"

"I don't know. Maybe the spring will come."

LIBRA FOUNDATIONS IS like any other brotherhood of white-collar kingpins.

First I tell the board that the thief is a level-eight employee.

Then they have to decide, before I reveal who he is, if they'd really want to prosecute one of their elite corporate-officer-types. Gene's no departmental president or even vice president, but he's a protégé of one kind or another and they have to weigh out office politics.

Libra tells me they'll call next week for the offender's name.

A week's worth of suspense might just raise my rates.

IT'S BEEN five days since Persephone came to visit, and I find myself thinking of her.

While the corporate fraternity is making up its mind on Gene, I've started on another case. Classic gumshoe work: *Is my husband cheating on me?*

Generally boring stuff, but it pays the bills.

And based on my half-hour meeting with Mrs. Richards, my guess would be: *Yes, bitch, he is.*

I imagine living with that woman would drive any man to drink, so why not go home with the barmaid while you're at it?

I'M WALKING down Ernest Street, midday. Mr. Richards is a sales rep for Philosopher's Stone Pharmaceuticals. He's supposed to be at a convention in Denver.

At least that's what he told his wife.

But he's still here in town and walking just half a block ahead of me. And while the streets are busy today, his vat-grown red hairpiece is easy to keep track of.

That word sticks in my mind: *vat-grown.*

She's not even real—Persephone, I mean.

Just a dressed-up fallatio machine. Grown in some lab, stuffed with car parts, and tweaked to make her crave pre-baby goo instead of pureed baby food.

That hurts.

The pang of guilt is like a knot in my stomach, like swallowing gallstones.

It isn't her fault. And she isn't like that, just a machine. She sure as hell feels human. Her eyes are sure human enough.

Damn, listen to me.

I'm supposed to be hard-boiled.

Damn, have I lost Richards?

No. There he is, waiting to cross the street.

I pause, lean back against the wall of a dermal dye

shop. The sign reads: "Deepest beauty starts with your skin!" and "Image is everything!"

I try to apply that to Persephone: if she looks human maybe she is, or close enough.

Then again, maybe it's just a shallow damn slogan trying to sell skin dye.

Looking around, my gaze passes over another set of eyes. A man stares at me for a long moment, then looks away.

Not too slick.

Not much neck, either. Tall, thickly built, wearing a sleeveless electric T-shirt of alternating colors. Looks familiar...

The traffic light changes.

Cars stop, Richards goes.

So do I.

So does my new friend behind me.

Richards skips up a flight of stairs into a one-hour liposuction clinic. I wonder if he's getting sucked out or sucked off?

There's a rat-stick cart on the same block and I haven't had lunch yet. "One with mustard, please."

In the crowd of passersby, I see the radiating colors of the broad-chested T-shirt—green, yellow, red—glowing beneath a stern face. He's stopped too, and staring at me. Hard eyes, goatee...

Now I recognize him. It's one of the dolls Gene was showing me, an Aegis Crown, bodyguard model. Looks like this one's set on thug-mode.

"Gene, you son of a bitch," I mutter aloud.

I toss the rat-stick and start walking. I can pick up this lead on Richards later; right now I'd like to lose this tail.

I dodge down an alley, pop back up on another block. Cross the street.

The doll is still on me. Must be tweaked to be part bloodhound. And he's closing the gap, getting closer with each step.

I duck through a glass door, my brain registering the name as I go in: *Thursdays on Mother Earth.*

Inside is a foyer where shoes and flip-flops have been kicked to the side. Beyond a yellow bead curtain is a New Bohemian coffee shop. The lights are low and the air is thick, smelling of reefer and incense, coffee and body stink.

It's almost enough to choke on.

There are booths around the walls, a few patrons here and there, a coffee counter to my right, and a small center stage. A guy with braided whiskers plays a bluesy clarinet while a skinny blonde dances like an Egyptian snake. She's naked except for the blue and green serpents painted up and down her body. Her dirty hair is bundled into dreadlocks down to her ass and an inverted pyramid has been painted between her hips where there should be a triangle of hair.

My tail comes in when I'm barely through the beads.

His shirt is flashing from yellow to red, the colors reflected in his hard eyes. I came in here stupidly assuming that the doll has tact, that he won't jump me in a crowded afternoon coffee shop.

I'm wrong.

His fist sets my jaw crooked and sends me reeling. I stumble backward and knock over a six-armed Hindu goddess smoking incense sticks.

The statue shatters on the floor, lending sound effects to the next fist against my face.

I fall into the musician, swipe the clarinet from his hand and crack it upside the doll's head.

A few of the broken keys cling to his face, then fall off. Aegis looks pissed.

I duck and the musician takes a hit for me, giving me time to roll around and come up with the spacer in hand.

He isn't impressed, doesn't even blink.

So I pull the trigger.

A swarm of tiny darts burst from the wide-mouthed barrel and imbed themselves in the doll's face. Little blue arcs of electricity dance randomly across the net. He blinks...

Then shakes it off.

Damn thing has a synthetic nervous system. The stun gun doesn't work.

His fist crushes my nose.

He hits me in the guts, doubling me over. Knee to my chin, a hard shove. I'm thrown onto my back, onto the stage.

Through the stars in my vision, I see the naked dancer, her legs chopping frantically, not sure what to do.

"Well don't just stand there, bitch," I grumble aloud, grabbing an ankle and yanking it out from under her.

She falls right on top of the doll and latches on, screaming. I hope she can hold him for a more than a second.

I spit blood, slide to my feet, and quickly hobble over to the coffee counter. The tattooed java-slinger is more than happy to get out of my way and it takes me only a blink to find a potential weapon: an old-fashioned, metal coffee pot. I toss the lid, unplug it, and grab it by both handles.

The caffeinated hippies groan as the dancer hits the floor.

The tattooed girl yelps and dives over the far side of the counter.

I spin to find Aegis tearing toward me, his face all wadded up and swollen, full of scratch marks and taser darts.

I add hot coffee to the mess.

His electric T-shirt shorts out, sparks to a neutral plastic grey. His mouth gapes in a silent scream.

Then I slam his jaw shut with the broadside of the percolator.

He's still standing, so I hit him again, and then with the backswing.

His ear has come loose and hangs from his head by thin strands.

The rabble of shop patrons get to their feet now, one by one, each made braver by the last. Their filthy mouths bear teeth and cheer, their bloodshot eyes glisten.

I flip the coffee pot over, draw back with both hands, and drive it onto the doll's head. It jams halfway so I force it, shearing off his other ear.

The fleshy disk drops on the floor.

No blood, I notice.

An instant later, pinpricks of sky blue foam rise to the surface.

"She'd bleed," I tell him.

Persephone would bleed. I'm sure of it.

I give the now blind, kettle-headed robot a shove into the throng of worked-up, stoned-out caffeine hippies who tear into him like the starving masses on Arena Day.

<hr>

REMOTE HACKING the key codes to Gene's apartment is easy. I wait for night to fall, then go visiting. The doorman is an occasional informant of mine and lets me in with a nod.

Twenty-second floor.

Polished chrome walls, reproductions of old paintings in the hallway.

No point to listening at the door, these places are all soundproofed for maximum privacy; no matter what loud, sick shit these ritzy fat cats are into, they keep it to themselves.

I have the spacer in my pocket and a real gun in hand, a classic snubnosed .38 revolver. Fits my style and, if your aim is good, it's as effective on dolls as people.

I patter in the key code and go in quiet.

The living room is huge, big bay windows set to opaque, circular couch bigger than my office, chrome liquor cabinet in the corner, lights low. One entire wall is a vidscreen on mute with some low-budget porno running. No bodyguard dolls in sight.

Gene probably figures the first one took care of me.

Sealed door on my right, hallway to the left.

Grunting to the left.

I feel my skin tingle, some green flash of jealousy I'm ashamed to admit is there. My hands are even sweating.

I give the revolver a reassuring squeeze.

The hall is dark. Purple light shines from a far room,

the source of the sex noise. I creep down with my gun at the ready, then spin into the doorway.

My sights level on Gene: plump, naked, and tied to the four posts of his king-sized canopy bed. Lying comfortably next to him is...

Persephone?

His naked companion sits up, hair short and purple and matted together in sticky ropes. Her skin is dark and mottled, a moody blue in this light.

She sees me and throws herself across Gene's vulnerable body. "No!" she croaks. "No, he's mine!"

There's no one else in the room. Just a big automated wardrobe and an oversized padded chair. The purple light shines from a long thin lamp on the wall.

I dial it up to white.

The girl is still blue.

This isn't Persephone. This one looks... underdeveloped, incomplete. Her skin has an artificial sheen to it, like stretched rubber, colored in varying shades of indigo. Her areola and nipples are blotchy and oversized. Eyes are mostly white, the irises colorless. One ear is visible through the thick purple strands of what would become hair, though it's little more than an irregular bump on the side of her head.

She holds up one hand, warding me off, fingers webbed.

"Harry!" Gene screams. "Harry, thank God! Get me out of here."

This isn't his kinky fantasy come true.

Gene's a prisoner. He's strapped down naked, his little cock worked raw.

"He's mine," the girl declares, voice gurgling. "I love him. I need him."

I relax, give a grin.

"What happened, lover boy? In too big a hurry to replace your tainted goods? Looks like maybe you tweaked this one a bit too much, popped her out of the oven a little too soon."

"Harry, *please!*"

"Why'd you do it, Gene? Why'd you send that thug after me? Was it because I was going to turn you in to Libra or was it because of Persephone?"

"Harry, you're my friend, I would never—"

"Cut the bullshit."

He cries out, voice dry and scratchy. "She was mine, you son of a bitch! I made her for *me!* And you took her. Ain't seen me in ten years and you come right in and take my girl. *Again!* I hate you, Harry Celeste, *hate you!*"

"Where's Persephone?" I move closer, so he can see my gun.

The girl crouches over him on all fours, like a mother leopard.

"You get me out of here," he says, "and I'll tell you."

"Tell me first."

"I locked her in the kitchen. Yesterday morning."

The sealed door.

I use the same key code and it opens.

The room is dark, lit only by the flickering bulb in the open refrigerator. The shelves of the fridge have been torn out, food spilled out across the floor. Among the shadows I see a table, some stools, counter tops.

No girl.

Then something moves in one dark corner.

"Harry?"

I hear Persephone slide against the wall, getting to her feet. She stumbles into the light and falls into my arms, still in the vest and skirt from last week. An empty jar of baby food slips from her hand.

"Eating in the Underworld again?" I whisper, though she managed to change the menu.

Maybe I'll buy her dinner this time, somewhere sunny.

I kiss her cheek. She smells good, like a woman.

"We're leaving," I tell her.

Gene is bellowing from the bedroom. "Harry, get me out of here! I'm sorry. We're friends, for God's sake. After all these years, you're still my friend!"

"When the board asks who's been stealing their money," I call back, "I'll tell them where they can find you."

We seal the door behind us, locking Gene in his sound-proof *paradise*.

Persephone leans on me down the hall.

In the elevator, I hold her.

THE PROPOSAL

James stepped off the curb on Bleaker Street and stuck his hand in the air to hail a cab. A checkered yellow Studebaker drove past him, paying him no mind. In the back seat was an exotic looking woman in a broad-brimmed hat and pearls.

She looks nice, James thought to himself. *Guess I wouldn't have stopped either.*

Then again, I have Pauline. So I wouldn't have picked up that high-priced dame in the first place.

Pauline wasn't like most women James knew. Oh, she had all the feminine qualities that others had. She had beauty: curly raven locks, crystal blue eyes, and the curves of a rather short hourglass. She had brains: the mind of a university professor, the knowledge of a librarian, and the adventurous heart of an archeologist. And she fragility. She was a soft flower, drawn into a tight bulb most of her life, just now beginning to open up and blossom into womanhood.

James wasn't the only one to notice Pauline's own

personal spring, either, but he was right there. At her side. Working together, exploring together. He was her sun, she his rose. And though he was six years her senior, they were meant to be together. He was sure of it, and certainly she was, too.

Even though there had never been any actual, blatant expression of romantic feelings between them... Well, he knew it was true. *Certainly* she shared that unspoken bond.

Another cab passed him by, this one with no passenger in the back seat. It simply didn't stop for him.

James shifted the bundle of white daisies (he couldn't afford a dozen roses, not on a research assistant's stipend) from his left hand to his right, as well as the tiny wooden box he held.

Wait. Fragility? Pauline?

James chuckled. Would a fragile flower of a girl have survived that whole big scaffolding collapsing out from under her? The sarcophagus and weight of ages falling on top of her?

He saw the whole terrible scene again in his mind. Pauline, stout and curvy, in her working apron and flat-bottomed shoes, ten feet aloft on that bamboo scaffold. The stone chamber was lit by torches, flickering shadows everywhere. The huge stone mural of hieroglyphics loomed three-stories tall. Pauline was armed only with a coarse, horse-hair brush against the fearsome fate that was about to befall her. She swept away the dust and stones, clearing the negative space that spelled out some-thing important in standing figures and balancing cranes and swimming crocodiles. A warning, she had said. Pauline was reading it, translating it, as she went, and she had called his attention because she thought she had finally figured out what had been worth so much time and effort on the part of Egyptians two-thousand years dead.

And then it happened. The wall cracked, spontaneously broke open, and the sarcophagus spilled forth from its hiding place into the dim torch light. It practically landed on top of her, though in his mind's eye he still swore that the scaffolding had buckled first; Pauline was already in the act of falling when the vessel that would carry its cargo into the afterlife appeared from the crumbling wall.

Although that didn't make much sense. If not the weight of the coffin and rubble, what would have caused such a thing to happen?

The scaffold, the opening sarcophagus, and Pauline, all piled up on the tomb floor. A wave of dust roiled outward. James had been so frightened that his eyes had played tricks on him. He swore that he saw faces in that thundercloud of dust and debris. A beautiful woman one instant, a withered, cackling skull in the next, there and gone in the space of a blink as the particles hit him in the face. He had already hurtled himself into the chaos, was tasting and choking on the airborne remains of a deceased priestess and ages of lost history.

That had been the end of the expedition. Pauline— poor lovely, delicate Pauline—had suffered bodily injury and was unconscious as he carried her from the cavernous tomb. The guides and their camels, supposedly waiting for them outside, were in the act of fleeing when he emerged carrying his burden of love. Had he been a moment later in making it to sands and sky, he and Pauline would have been trapped there, alone. He'd have held her in his arms and watched her slowly die there in the deserts east of Cairo.

James's heart reacted again—speeding up, pounding against his ribs, the green taste of dread surging up his throat, thinking the girl he loved but had never told so had just been killed before his very eyes. His hands tightened involuntarily, crunching the green flower stalks and testing the sturdiness of the small wooden cube.

After a brief hospital stay in Cairo, they were flown back home to the States. James went to his lonely apartment, and back to the university to deliver their treasures and report his findings to the board of regents. Pauline went to Gothic General. There she slept in the care of physicians and nurses who couldn't say what was wrong with her. She appeared to suffer no serious injuries, and yet was oblivious to the world. Comatose.

Until today. When James had phoned the hospital today, they'd told him that Pauline had woken up and discharged herself from their care. The doctors could see no reason to hold her, as she'd spontaneously awoken from the only ailment with which they could charge her.

But why did James have to find out this way? Why hadn't Pauline telephoned him to assist her home? Or invited him to see her once she was safely back to her apartment?

Had her deep, death-like sleep robbed her of the feelings she once held for him? (For, surely, she loved James as much as he did her. Surely, her endless fever dreams were fantasies about their finally professing their undying love for one another, and about their wedding day, and their future children.)

Finally, a yellow cab declaring itself of the Acme Taxi Service eased to a stop next to where James stood in the street. The driver's face must have been a reflection of James's own flustered, hopeful, and heartbroken expression, for he gave him quite an inquisitive and puzzled look.

James gave the cabbie the address, following with, "My girl's just been released from the hospital. We are reuniting today after nearly two weeks apart."

"Congratulations, mac," the driver said. "But, in that case, don't you think you could have sprung for roses?"

Eighteen minutes later, the cab deposited James outside her building.

But he wasn't the only one there waiting.

A swarm of cats, dogs, pigeons, and even rats were amassed at the stairwell door.

The cabbie sped away with curses of confusion and disgust. James stood at the edge of the street, gripping his gifts, half afraid to step up on the curb. Several of the beasts turned around to stare him down. A mangy hound and a fierce Dachshund growled at him. More than a few cats hissed in his direction—not at the rats or canines, their natural enemies, but seemingly at James.

Finally a jet-feathered rook squawked at him, perched on a lamppost above his initial field of vision. It cawed again and the savage peanut gallery cowered. The black bird flicked its head from side to side, sizing James up with one eye and then the other. He had the strange feeling that he was being assessed for worthiness. James fidgeted with his bowtie.

Suddenly a Roadster blew past him, blaring its horn. James jumped onto the sidewalk.

The menagerie of creatures gathered there, however, did not budge. They flipped around en mass to face him, to keep him from reaching the door. Only when the rook fluttered down among them, hopped around and swept its wings in shooing arcs did they take the hint and move aside. A few seconds later, the way was cleared. The animals had all retreated to the open alleyway, crouching around the corner, or peeked on from behind a blue postal box. Then the winged usher flew back to its perch and squawked a final time, as if to order James inside.

"Damnedest thing I've ever seen in my short life-time..." James muttered, hurrying through the door and mounting the first few steps in a single bound.

Pauline's apartment was number 2B. He had never been there, but he knew it from the university records. And she must have told him herself once, as well. He was certain she would have.

James cleared his throat, smoothed his hair, and checked his bowtie one more time. He inspected his daisies and found one stalk fractured and drooping where he'd clutched it too tightly. That one he tossed, primped the rest, and poised his fist to knock.

But the door eased open of its own accord, just enough to allow her bid to enter to reach the hallway.

"Um, hello?" he called, gently pushing open the door. "Pauline? It's James. Come, uh, come a-calling. Of a sort."

Her apartment was small but nice. The foyer merged with the parlor on the left and kitchenette on the right. There was a sea-green sofa and chair in the parlor. A Zenith radio sat on a small, circular table beneath the window.

Something black uncoiled itself on one seafoamcolored pillow. A black Persian cat lifted its head, probing him with yellow eyes and pointed ears. The thick furball climbed up into a sitting position and glared on, watching him defensively.

"Oh, you have a cat," James said nervously. "You never mentioned that before."

"I always keep one vassal close," came Pauline's voice, rougher and more determined than he was used to hearing, "and several more in waiting."

She strutted into the parlor and went immediately the Persian, stroking its head between the ears. She looked... good, he supposed. Pauline stood slightly taller than he remembered, wearing a strapless blue dress, black sandals, and what must have been every piece of jewelry she owned. He recognized some, simple necklaces and a few inexpensive rings that she'd inherited from her grandmother, she'd said. But Pauline usually went modest on her adornments. Today, seven fingers wore rings of various styles and the pale, bare skin of her chest held almost as many chains, lockets, and brooches. A thin tiara was poked into her curly raven hair with interlaced triangular silverwork centered at her forehead.

Her face... Her face was pale, too, cheekbones more pronounced, and her eyes appeared sunken, made worse by the darkening application of cosmetic eyeshadow and thick, ruby lip gloss. Pauline almost never wore make-up, and he'd certainly never seen her put it on so heavily.

Two weeks asleep, he reasoned. *Not eating, not taking care of herself, just... Just the illness. And two weeks of famine. That must be it.*

Pauline glared at him. "Well?" she demanded.

"Well, uh," James stammered. "I wish you'd have telephoned me, Pauline, I could have helped you home."

"Are those for me?" she asked expectedly.

"Oh, yes!" He clumsily stumbled forward, flowers outstretched. When she didn't take the bouquet, he simply lowered his arm. The tiny wooden cube he gripped even tighter now, consuming it in his hand. He almost hoped she didn't see it, that he hadn't brought it.

"So, uh, how are you feeling?"

"Better," she said. "Better than I have in years. Thousands and thousands of years."

James chuckled. "It's only been two weeks. Two long weeks, granted. They seemed a lifetime to me, too." He felt his cheeks blush and hated himself for it.

"Oh, the treasures!" He looked around for somewhere to place the flowers, found nothing, and continued. "The tomb, the artifacts, everything we brought back from Cairo."

"Oh, Cairo," she breathed. "Poor ignorant, vengeful Cairo..."

"Uh, yes. Well... Not sure what you mean there, dear." He'd slipped in a *dear!* Had she even noticed? Did she mind? "Professor Clark has analyzed what we found and determined that the tomb belonged to an excommunicated priestess—"

"Hecateptra," Pauline said, stepping nearer. "The Stillness of the Water. The Emptiness of the Night. The Cold in Men's Hearts."

She was close now—*very* close, inches from him. A dark passion flared in the deepness of her blue eyes. Her ruby lips pursed provocatively as she formed each syllable. She stood so near to him now that the heat of her body... Well, actually, he felt a rather chill vacuum coming from her direction, but James certainly felt warmer.

He flushed and licked his lips with a suddenly dry and anxious tongue.

"That's right," he whispered.

Her fathomless blue gaze locked on to his. He felt as if he were swimming in those dark pools.

Swimming.

Sinking.

Drowning.

Her powerful, entrancing glare broke away and glanced downward.

"What do you have there? What are you keeping secret from me?"

Slowly, he raised his hand and unfurled his fingers. A tiny wooden box, two cubic inches, rested on his palm. He dropped the daisies to the floor and used his other hand to slide open the lid. Inside, nestled among a packing of shredded paper, was a ring. A scarab of tarnished turquoise, hastily polished as best he could, clasped to a circlet of pure gold.

"Ah," she said. "My ring. After all these long years of slumber, you've found it for me."

James nodded wordlessly. It seemed to him that he'd wanted to say quite a bit more about the ring when he'd come in, but those thought were all lost now. His tongue lay idle and nothing came to mind. He was lost within himself. And soon, he somehow knew, everything else would be lost, too.

"I'll be happy to reclaim it. But, my dear..." Her cold,

clammy hand with its bright red fingernails caressed his cheek. "Why don't you kneel for me?"

The chill of her touch shuddered through his entire body, settling like frost in his joints and in his heart. James lowered himself silently, planting his left knee on the floor—right on top of the bouquet of daisies—and held the ancient scarab in its box aloft.

"Thank you, my love," she purred, staring down on him. "With this ring, I claim you, and this world, as my own."

UNFEELING

"Somebody needs to get a mop in there," Shovel says, thumbing back at the men's room. The pretty boy bartender just stares for a second. Maybe he doesn't catch the words over the pulsing music, but he can read the meaning in Shovel's dark, unfeeling eyes. When a brick of clay in a black suit says get a fucking mop, you better know why.

Byrd's at the bar. He's relatively new to the outfit and already trying to set himself a place at the big boys' table. Shovel would rather just walk past him, but instead pauses to look Byrd in the eye.

That cocky look is there; it's always there.

"You know why they call you 'Shovel?'" he asks, then takes a long gulp on his vodka and cranberry. He can't even drink like a man.

"You know why they call you 'Byrd?'"

Skinny prick looks like a bird: tall and thin, reed-like legs, long neck, feathery blond hair.

But it's also his name, so Byrd just smiles and laughs

it off, then finishes what he was saying: "It's 'cause you get all the *shit* jobs."

More giggles, like a little girl, like a loony bird.

"No," Shovel says. "It's because I generally don't give a damn either way." He leans in close enough to smell the expensive cologne Byrd's wearing. "But I don't like you."

There's a half-smile frozen on the loony's face for a few seconds, trying to decide if it's a joke or not. It isn't, but he laughs anyway.

"Laugh it up," Shovel grumbles, walking away.

George is still at the table with the boss, his white suit glowing under the club's funky lights. The boss looks even whiter, his face pale and glistening.

Shovel and George share a look. They aren't used to seeing him like this. August Alexander practically runs this town and he's *never* nervous, but tonight, he's all jangly.

It's a semi-circular booth and George slides in for Shovel.

August about comes across the table. "Did you get it?"

There's a desperation in his eyes that was never there before. August was known for his blue eyes, his icy stare. Hell, it's half of what got him where he is today. And now that cold resolve has gone missing, and so has some of the respect Shovel's always had for him.

"Of course I got it."

The man in the john—Dim, they call him—had two things that August Alexander had decided he wanted. Now Dim's lying in a mess of his own blood, wedged between the toilet and the divider with his pants around his ankles. And why? Because he had a little wooden doll and the attention of a particular woman. Only the

Devil knows why the boss wants them, but they're his now.

Shovel sets his meaty paw on the table and opens it.

Inside is a simple wooden carving not three inches tall, a bell-shaped head with a bell-shaped body. It looks like a woman in a dress with no arms or legs. There are two dots with eyelashes and a low V-neck, all in red paint.

Not very artistic. A fifth-grader could pull this off.

August snatches it from the thick palm, holds it up in the flashing dance floor light, then kisses the damned thing.

"Go call her," he orders. Confidence has returned to the surface but his eyes show the same helpless desperation clawing at him underneath. "Call her and tell her I want to see her tonight. Tell her Dim's out of the picture. She's August's girl now."

Shovel and George don't stir right away. Obviously neither of them approve, but the boss is the boss.

"Go on!" he shouts.

His boys inch out of the booth and make their way toward the bar. They look like opposites, one dressed in black, one in white, but they're more like brothers. They talk about their love-struck father.

"I don't get it," Shovel shouts over the music.

"Neither do I," George replies. "I mean, I get what's in it for her. Gold-diggers always want to be a big man's woman. And August don't even mind the gold-diggers, till they start thinking they own a piece of it. Hell, I don't even mind them telling me what to do once in a while, if they're nice looking. But this one..."

Shovel grunts in agreement.

He's seen this Elisa once: pushing fifty, crows feet, flat-chested, homely. The boss usually hits the town with a big-busted twenty-year-old on his arm. But August Alexander isn't the first big man this woman has sunk her claws into. Shovel heard she was seeing a local rock star for a while and that she'd appeared in the gossip column with her arm twisted around some millionaire.

"Weird bitch must have something going for her," Shovel says, "but damned if I know what it is."

They reach the bar where Byrd is leaning against it all suave, talking to some girl with big hair.

George and Shovel step in on either side of Byrd, George between him and the girl, and he says loud enough for all of them, "All I can think is she must give one hell of a blow job."

Then he turns to her, smiles, and tells her to beat it.

"Hey," Byrd snaps, "I'm working here!"

Shovel places one big mitt on his shoulder and tells him to go sit with the boss.

"What, old Double-A can't be left alone?" More jokes, more giggling. "What is he, Macaulay-Fucking-Culkin?"

"Just do it," George says.

Then, to the bartender, "Give me a phone."

A young kid in an apron goes by, pushing a mop bucket. He struggles to get it inside the men's room while holding the door with one foot.

Shovel gives the club a quick glance to see if Dim's still walking around, bloody-lipped and looking for more trouble. No sign of him.

George hangs up the phone and gives his friend a disappointed look. "Her majesty says that'll be fine."

They head back to the table where Byrd's eyeing the women and August is studying the doll. He looks up when the pair sit down, forcing the new guy to slide all the way around.

"Well?"

George nods. "Yeah, boss, she says she'd be delighted to see you tonight. Her place around midnight, she says."

"And this loser Dim?"

"She didn't even mention him."

"He won't be back," Shovel assures him. "I made sure he knew the score."

THE BOSS SEES no further reason to hang out at the Black Cat. He wants to go home and, "You know," he says, his hands fluttering, "freshen up. Don't look at me like I'm some bitch on Oprah, let's just get out of here."

The pecking order in the car is standard: George drives, the boss rides shotgun, and Shovel and Byrd ride in the back. The valet brings the Caddie around and everyone starts to climb in, but August takes Byrd's seat and tells him to sit in the front. There's a moment of confusion at this sudden change in protocol, but they're soon on their way.

Byrd runs the music too loud to talk, which is fine; the boss isn't in the habit of explaining himself anyway and no one wants to ask.

About halfway back to the house, August grabs Shovel's idle hand and gives it a squeeze, kind of a *you're my main man* gesture. Shovel, as expressionless as ever, just gives the boss a single nod.

Once they're back at the house, he finds out why.

"I don't trust them anymore," August tells him.

They're in the master bedroom, which is about as big as Shovel's whole damn apartment. George and Byrd are downstairs, checking out the car and getting everyone something to eat, respectively, as instructed. August is standing in the middle of his closet holding up various neckties in the mirror.

"You're the only one I can trust with her. Shovel the Unfeeling, the human instrument. A man with no emotion, no fear, no regret. Your reputation made your career, and mine. You're solid as a rock. But those other two…"

He decides on a cobalt blue tie, silk. "Good with my eyes, eh?" he says, knowing he'll get no reply.

"Those other two, they might get jealous. Can't have that. That's why I need it to be just you and me from now on. You'll manage the other crews but keep them at a distance. You, me, and her, from now on."

"I don't think I understand," Shovel says.

"Get rid of them."

Shovel gives August a look, one that only he and George can get away with.

"Boss… Byrd's just a splatter of shit on the windshield. I don't mind giving him the heave-ho and busting his beak for good measure. But George has been with you a long time. Longer than me. He's as loyal—"

"As loyal as a dog," August snarls. "And as soon as the right bitch comes in heat, he'll turn on me and try to take her for himself. No. Things are changing."

"Maybe you should take the night to think about this,

August. Don't see what's-her-name tonight, just have a sandwich and a drink and get some sleep."

That famous icy glare returns with cold fire behind it.

August's finger rises an inch from Shovel's flat nose.

"Don't you back talk *me*. You get your ass downstairs and do your fucking job. Get rid of them, before they get rid of me.

"And I don't want them coming back for me later, you hear? *Get rid of them.*"

Shovel's name and rep are well founded: he's a neutral instrument.

He FINDS Byrd working on the big island in the kitchen, mayo and mustard jars without lids, three kinds of deli meat unwrapped from white butcher paper, two lengths of Italian bread.

He has a foot-long knife in his hand and has just made a mess of the first loaf, cutting it jagged, crumbs everywhere. He's about to saw the next one when Shovel comes in.

Byrd gives a frustrated shrug and complains about getting the goddamn maid's job.

Shovel sets a meaty paw over the loony's knife hand.

Suddenly Byrd doesn't mind being the sandwich bitch but, hey, sure, you can finish it if you like. He lets Shovel have the big knife and takes a step back.

Shovel's dull shark's eyes stare at him.

"You were right. I do get all the shit jobs."

He clamps onto Byrd's throat, whose bulging eyes threaten to pop from their sockets. Byrd's manicured hands tug at Shovel's wrist but can't budge it, so he goes for the eyes.

Shovel's bread knife slashes defensively.

Byrd's knees buckle and Shovel has to hold him up by the throat. The weight requires an even tighter grip, squeezing all the strength out of those slapping, bloody hands.

"As if the girl would want you anyway," Shovel says.

It's as close to an apology as he gives before wringing out the last of Byrd's life.

When it's over, Shovel drags the body into the corner, kicks him down low among the cabinets, and wipes his hands on a dish towel on his way outside.

THE SCREEN DOOR SLAMS.

George is in the garage, his white sports coat hanging on a hook, shirt sleeves rolled up. He peeks over the raised hood of the Cadillac and is reinserting the dipstick when Shovel comes around to the front of the vehicle. There's not much space here between the bumper and the tool bench, not much room to struggle and no where to run.

Shovel picks up a big wrench.

George is shaking his head. "Oil's fine, tranny fluid, I even topped off the damn windshield washer tank. I don't know what the hell I'm supposed to be looking for out here. This is bullshit, checking the car in the middle of the night."

Shovel nods in agreement.

"The man's losing it, you know. This woman's got him going crazy."

"I know," Shovel says, his face expressionless.

"I hope he doesn't expect me to drive him over there. I can find better things to do than sit in the car while he gets laid."

"He doesn't."

Shovel closes in. George tries to back up but can't—the tool bench is there.

Shovel's wrench catches him in the nose on the up-swing and stuns him. A left hook throws him backward, then a big paw grips the back of his head and twists him into a headlock, choking off his air.

"*What*—" George gasps, red sputtering from his lips, "*what*—, *what*—"

"You're right," Shovel explains, "he's gone nuts. Old Blue Eyes has been taken over by the green-eyed monster."

George tries to struggle but Shovel's got him; there *is* no struggle.

"He's gone deep-end jealous and I'm the only one he trusts. Because I'm such a damned unfeeling brute."

The lethal arm relaxes and George spills to the concrete, gasping for breath.

Shovel hovers over him a moment more, then gives him room.

"Something is different," he says, but more to himself.

Everything's turned upside-down because of this strange bitch. Even Shovel's beginning to *feel* something.

His friend rests on the cold floor, white tie all askew, red spots on his collar.

"You have to go. Leave town, George."

George is still panting, too confused to be angry. "This is crazy!"

"Yes."

"I been with him years..." The color comes back into George's face. Now he looks scared. "What about Byrd?"

"Byrd's already dead."

This convinces him.

They say goodbye and Shovel starts back to the house.

He feels it on his back, like eyes watching him, that possibility of George coming from behind, putting two slugs in him and then going up to finish off that traitor, Alexander. Shovel really doesn't care either way, he'd almost welcome it. But it doesn't happen.

TWENTY MINUTES LATER, when he and August are leaving, Shovel walks around to the front of the car and finds nothing but a wrench on the floor. He slams the hood shut and climbs into the driver's seat.

"Where are they?" the boss wants to know.

Shovel backs out of the driveway with his arm behind August's seat. "They're in the trunk," he says flatly. "I'll get rid of them after I drop you off."

"Good." August has arrested the rearview mirror and is checking himself out. "Then come back and wait in the driveway. I don't want us unprotected, in case that Dim comes by."

Anger flares inside Shovel. Didn't he say Dim knew the score? Didn't he already take care of that?

Shovel the Unfeeling is getting a little hot, even fiery, when he sees the doll again.

That stupid fucking doll.

August takes it out of his pocket and stares at it lovingly.

I should have kept the damned thing, Shovel says to himself. *I'm the one who went and got it, I'm the one who bloodied a man for it. More mine than his.*

It's just past midnight when they pull up to Elisa's gate.

The wrought iron swings open and the Cadillac eases up to the house. It's not a mansion, but it's nice. Her wealth, Shovel figures, has probably been accumulated from her many admirers. There's a fountain on the front lawn with a chubby young angel pouring water from a vase, foot lights shining up at it.

Shovel gets a better look as he's getting out of the car and decides that the cherub's face looks more spiteful than innocent.

"Where the hell do you think you're going?" August demands, slamming his car door.

"I'll walk you in," Shovel replies, his voice not so flat anymore. "I figured I killed two of my friends and beat the shit out of a man taking a dump to get you here, I might as well go all the way."

August doesn't argue, just leads the way to the front door. He rings the bell once and a woman's voice bids them to enter.

The foyer is big with a marble floor and columns. A skinny black cat slips between the two men and out the door, disappearing into the night. Their eyes follow it.

"Oh, don't worry about her," their hostess says.

Both men look up.

There she is, the bitch of the evening. The old crone that's caused this mess.

Seeing her in better light, she looks more like she's pushing sixty, thin as that cat, small droopy breasts, wearing a slinky black dress that shows off her knobby shoulders. Her hair is dyed hazel, her face well powdered and lips thick with blood red gloss. She looks like a whore who doesn't know when to retire.

Then again...

There *is* something sexy about this woman, something charming about the crow's feet crinkling at her eyes, the confident and mischievous smile like a cat who hasn't just eaten a canary but has a few more tied up in the closet for later.

Elisa holds out her arms as if to embrace them both.

"Gentlemen," she says, her voice like the soothing music in lunatic asylums. "What are we doing tonight?"

A warmth flashes over Shovel, something he's never felt before.

August is a step ahead of him, this dumb schoolboy crush on his slack-jawed face. Shovel sees the wooden doll peeking out of August's sweaty little hand.

Before he even knows why, Shovel is pummeling August Alexander, first a blow to the back of the head, then his face. He snatches a phone from a nearby table and clangs it against those famous blue eyes until they close and August's forehead splits and bleeds.

Finally the boss's flailing hand drops and the tiny doll spins away across the smooth marble.

She stops it with one slender foot and reaches down with long, red finger nails.

As Elisa curls back up, deliberately slow, Shovel can see inside the dress, breasts uninhibited by a bra, perhaps elongated by time but somehow still perky.

He wets his lips.

So does she.

"I don't understand," he says helplessly.

"The doll *belongs* to me," the woman purrs.

She holds it up so he can see the bell-shaped head, the blood-lashed eyes, the deep plunging V of the dress. Then her crimson lips kiss it. The head disappears inside, throbbed in and out quickly, erotically.

Shovel feels a response push against his pants.

She gives him a sexy grin, the wrinkles at her eyes like spider webs. "And so does anyone who touches it."

She holds out one claw-like hand.

"Now come to me."

MIME

It was just past midnight and there was a mime trapped in an invisible box behind Donatello's.

Pauli had just been commenting to Mouse how there had been a dumpster there a few years ago, back when this was a regular drop. But the dumpster was gone now, relocated because the police had found too many bad things in it, which was why Don's had been off the drop list for so long. The place was cold now, safe.

Except for the goofy painted street rat feeling out some ghostly prison where the dumpster used to be.

The mime smiled at Mouse and Pauli as they came out the back door. His face was white and his hair such a pale blond it looked like bleached bone, all contrasted by a red scarf and black leotard. He stood under the alleyway street lamp like it was a spotlight, waving now with one hand and propped against the air with the other.

The two men shared a look. "You think he saw anything?" the smaller man, Mouse, asked his friend.

"Saw what?" Pauli said, approaching the clown. "We're just two dish washers closing up late. Ain't that right, Smiley? You didn't see nothing, did you?"

The mime jerked his head back and forth like a cartoon character.

Both thugs laughed, though the humor died quickly as they crowded into the dim spotlight. All three stood within the ring, very close, very quiet.

Pauli folded his thick arms and glared.

Mouse smoked his cigarette, the red glow reflected in his steady eyes.

The mime just smiled lazily.

Mouse finally flicked the smoldering butt into the clown's chest. "What the hell you doing here this late?" he demanded.

The mime made a pillow of his white-gloved hands and laid his head there, asleep for a moment. Then his eyes popped open; even his eyes were almost white, so light was the grey of his irises. He straightened his neck and shook his head, as if disappointed.

"Couldn't sleep, eh?" Pauli slapped Mouse's shoulder with the back of his hand. "Hey, what do you know, I speak mime!"

Mouse looked the alley up and down but it was dark and empty, save their own silver Cadillac. "What'd you do, walk here? Ain't no houses 'round here, no buses running this late."

The mime made like he was running in place, stumbled and recovered, then shook his fist back at whatever invisible obstacle he'd just tripped over.

Pauli cracked up. "Oh, I think I like this guy."

"Yeah? Well I don't." Mouse groped him, feeling

around his skintight clothes, pinching the soft red fabric at his neck.

Pauli became serious. "You ain't wearing a wire on us now, are you, friend?"

The white face also became serious and moved in the negative. He drew an X over his heart and held up one hand.

"You know what would happen if you were?" Mouse asked.

One finger cut the air across his red scarf.

"That's right," Pauli said. Then he back-slapped Mouse's arm again. "Hey, you know who this guy reminds me of? Remember Lexi? Sexy Lexi? Thought he was a funny man."

Mouse rolled his eyes. "Yeah, he *thought* he was fucking funny. Don't miss that guy."

The mime thumbed at himself and shook his head, as if to say, *Me neither.* His face drew into deep frown, fingers fluttering down like tears from his eyes. He tugged at his legs, which were now fast to the ground. Then he started swaying, hands flat and rising to show the water level. The silent crying became mute pleas for mercy, until his fingers brushed his mouth and he blew up like a blowfish to keep from drowning. But he could only hold his breath so long. His grey-white eyes roamed to and fro, mouth finally popped, and he silently gasped in a death swallow of ethereal water.

Then he took a bow.

The two thugs shared a look.

"Yeah, that's right," Pauli said suspiciously. "Lexi's swimming with the fishes."

"Hey, Pauli, while we're strolling down memory lane,

you remember Tanner?" Mouse glanced around, then nodded upward at a nearby fire escape. "Might be a good night for remembering Tanner, eh?"

"Yeah, might not be a bad idea."

The mime held the tail of his scarf aloft and dropped his head, hanging dead, just like Tanner.

The next instant he was smiling casually again, pointing at himself and shaking his head: *You don't want to hang me like that.*

"You're pretty fucking smart for a homeless circus freak," Mouse growled.

"Think he's a cop?"

"Nah. This ain't no cop style. Maybe some wiseass, thinks he's got money coming. That it? You keep up the silent treatment if you get paid, is that what you think?"

The mime rolled his eyes at such a ridiculous idea.

Pauli leaned in close. "No, wait. You know who this guy really reminds me of? Whitey Brown." He gave the obligatory chuckle at the name. "Remember that albino fuck? Looks a lot like him."

"Except Brown's dead."

"Yeah," Pauli said, not quite sure.

The mime nodded in agreement and drew another invisible line across his throat.

The thugs' eyes met and decided on action.

Mouse seized their victim, twisted his arms to the rear and kicked the back of one knee. The mime dropped into a kneeling position.

Pauli pulled a switchblade.

"Fun's over, Smiley. You should know, I fucking hate mimes." He popped the knife and let the lamp light play on its edge. "Hey, Mouse, you know the best thing about killing a mime? No one hears him scream."

Pauli gave a humorless laugh and jerked the red scarf out of the way.

Beneath it, a fine bloodless slit gaped in the mime's throat.

The clown's eyes burned with new fire and a smile flashed on his face as a straight razor flashed in his hand.

No one heard Pauli or Mouse scream.

LONELY

Dead of night, kicked out of the bar when the lights came up. Paul moves quickly to the sidewalk, a bouncer right behind him. But he's not running from the big guy in the "STAFF" t-shirt, he's trying to catch those last few girls...

Damn.

Two of them scurry down the street together double-quick, giggling loudly. Maybe they saw him coming. The last girl, the blonde he'd watched come back for beer after beer—his last chance—is climbing into another guy's car.

The pink neon glow above the door goes dark.

Nothing left to do but go home, he tells himself.

But I don't want to, he answers. *At least not alone.*

Paul's car is one of two left in the lot down the street. The other one has flattening tires, doesn't look like it's moved in weeks. His VW bug starts up like it'd rather take a few weeks off, too. The trip across the country was hard on it.

Paul's rattling car slows down at a light, red and green cast down the empty streets. There's no sign of life, no traffic. He glides through the red.

Be careful, he tells himself afterward. *I'm too drunk to get pulled over for something stupid.*

A figure flashes by on the sidewalk, didn't notice her till it was too late. At least he thinks it was a her; that peripheral glimpse of white seemed feminine.

Paul finds his foot on the brake, his car turning around in the nearest parking lot, a field of black devoid of any other cars.

Am I really doing this? he thinks.

Better than another empty night alone.

There's a girl meandering around an alleyway: thin, blonde hair, white sun dress. He hugs the curb in the wrong lane and rolls down the passenger side window.

"Aren't you cold?" he calls out nervously.

She's dancing all by herself, does a spin that flares her short dress out, then stumbles around to look at him.

She must be drunker than I am, he thinks.

The girl catwalks to the car and leans down, letting the view of her small breasts hanging inside the dress linger a second before bringing her face down into the widow.

She's cute, short curly hair, dark eyes that shine in the dashboard light. Her lips are full, black lipstick smeared at the corners.

"Hi," she says.

"Hi."

"What did you ask me?"

Paul clears his throat. "Um, I asked if you were cold."

"Always," she says, smiling. "But it feels warm in

here." She reaches in, puts her palm against the heating vent. Her skin is pale, nails are black.

"Come on in," he says, voice trembling just a bit.

"Okay." She unlocks the door through the window and slides into the seat, all the warmth inside rushing out.

"Colder out there than I thought. I'm Paul."

"I'm yours," she says quietly, then looks away.

Paul isn't sure if he heard that right but takes his foot off the brake. The car starts rolling again.

He clears his throat and turns up the heat. They cross a block in uncomfortable silence.

"Where we going, Paul?"

"Well, not many places *to* go. All the bars are closed now."

He steals a glance at her, looks her up and down. Despite being almost starvation-thin, she has chubby sort of cheeks and her skin is almost as white as her dress. She and it look like maybe they could use a bath, but she smells of something sweet.

"Lilacs." The word just tumbles out of his mouth.

She looks at him, puzzled.

"You smell sweet, like lilacs, and the white ones are the sweetest kind. Which is funny, you know, 'cause you're kind of all—"

She smiles at him, dark eyes glittering as they pass under a street light.

All white except for the eyes, and lips, and nails... Her eyes have almost no whites to them at all.

"Sorry," he says, turning back to the road just in time for a stop sign. "My mom's a florist. I'm not like, way into flowers or anything, I'm just... A little drunk."

"Me too," she says, reaching over and squeezing his hand. Her touch is like ice. "If there's no where else to go, why not just go to your place?"

"Um, sure, we could do that," Paul says. "It'd certainly be warmer."

But she's too eager, he tells himself. *I'm not this lucky. She'd probably steal everything I own.*

His minds counters immediately: *Everything's still packed up. What's she going to do, carry heavy boxes down the street?*

"It's just down the street here. I guess I've been going that direction the whole time." He flashes her a nervous smile. "I just moved here, you know."

"From where?" She crosses her legs and plants an elbow on the armrest.

His hand checks the dial on the heater, assures him that it's turned up all the way.

"Iowa."

"*Iowa?*" she laughs. "I've never been there. Never been out of the city. Is it pretty?"

He looks at those chubby cheeks, those thick smudged lips, yellow curls hanging like overgrown vines, those glittering darks eyes. "Not as pretty as you."

Idiot! yells the voice in his head. *If you weren't so drunk you wouldn't have said something so stupid!*

She laughs, her voice like children at play.

"Thank you. That's definitely an Iowa thing to say, but sweet." She leans over, her pursed lips touch his cheek and he almost misses the turn.

The automated gate opens slowly then grinds closed behind them.

Around the back and up a flight of stairs is his front door. He fumbles with the keys.

"Wait," she says, taking his elbow and gently spinning him into a kiss. Their lips hold lightly for several seconds. When they part, her breath comes out like fog.

"Thank you," she whispers. "I've been so lonely."

Paul swallows. "Me too."

Inside is his small, dark apartment.

He reaches for the light switch but she places a hand over his. "No, I like it this way."

She dances into the living room as he tosses his jacket on the closet floor. The glow of night lights through the windows is enough to see by.

"Two empty bookshelves," she says, "a TV, and about a dozen cardboard boxes. At least you have a chair." She slides behind the big recliner, embraces it, then scratches her fingernails across the upholstery in a slow, seductive withdrawal. "I guess we could share it."

"Or," Paul says, "we could share the bed."

"Oh," she chirps, "there's a bed, too?" She takes his hand and lets him guide her into the bedroom.

The room's bare except for a mattress and box spring, dressed with sheets and a heavy quilt.

She pushes him down on it, straddles his legs, and pulls the white sun dress over her head. Underneath is nothing but her pale and imperfect skin: scratches on her shoulder and belly, a scar under her left breast. Her stomach is flat, a small divot for a navel; hips narrow, their bony crests visible. A thin stripe of blonde hair rises from between her legs.

His hands sweep over and cup her breasts, kneading

them as he kisses the cool skin below her sternum, then wraps his arms around her and tongues her nipples.

Their mouths lock together. Her tongue is like a scorpion tail, lashing in and out, striking and retreating.

She strips off his clothes, never away from his face for more than a few seconds, sucking his mouth and the very breath from him, then she's licking his ear, kissing his neck.

He shivers.

She slides into his lap, her knees up on the mattress, and he slides inside her. Her body seems to get colder and colder as they go, but now it's stimulating, like a dive into an icy pool. They fuck there on the edge of the bed in their carnal rhythm, both loud, moaning, panting...

PAUL OPENS HIS EYES, his body curled up on the edge of the mattress.

On the beige carpet is the red glow of the alarm clock: 5:23.

How long has he been asleep? Is she still here or has she slipped out and taken all his valuables with her?

No, Paul thinks. *I can feel her.*

Something cold is sharing the bed with him, a void draining the heat from the room, drawing it right out of his body. He realizes that this is what woke him up, the desperate need for a blanket.

He pauses for moment, listening for breathing, hears nothing and rolls over.

She's there next to him: petite, fragile, pale, and peacefully asleep. Blonde curls dangle in front of her face. He closes in on her, almost resting his head on the same pillow. Her lips are closed, black make-up streaked all over her mouth, nose small and still: no noise of breathing.

"Are you alive?" he whispers.

Shark's eyes pop open as if she'd never been asleep, reflecting the feeble moonlight. Her tongue licks the air, glistening black. "I'm hungry for you, Paul."

She rolls over and on top of him and bites into the side of his neck.

Paul yelps like a stricken dog and struggles underneath her but the girl centers her hips over his, thin legs slithering around him like constrictors. She squeezes his wrists and pins them to the bed, her skinny little frame twice as strong as he is.

Savage teeth penetrate deeper into his flesh and spread frost into his veins. He tries to scream but nothing comes out.

The girl rises slowly. Red strings of slobber bridge her face to his neck, then break and dangle from her chin.

"Oh, Paul," she purrs. "You taste so good."

He kicks with his whole body but she holds on, giggling.

He bucks again, shoulders, hips, legs, inching nearer to the edge of the bed.

"What's wrong, lover?"

Her messy mouth falls toward him again.

Paul bucks one last time and they slide off the mattress together, tumbling over. He breaks free and is on top now, delivers two rapid punches to the face, crack of bone on bone with the second, his knuckles against her cheek. Black-painted talons rake his face, cutting like dull razors.

Paul jumps backward onto his feet, barely out of reach as she swipes at him again. He collides with the wall, stumbles through the dark and out of the bedroom, bumps into an empty bookshelf and almost knocks it over.

The predator follows. Two pinpricks of white fire appear in the bedroom threshold.

A loose shelf plank cracks against her face. The sound is hollow and wet, like hitting a hard melon.

Paul draws back for another swing.

She's stunned for a second, blinks it off and turns her glare on him, bloody mouth in a bestial snarl.

He cracks her again.

And again.

She stumbles back into the bedroom with a panther-like whine.

The apartment door is right there, one step away.

He fumbles with the deadbolt, shaky hand working too fast to be accurate.

She snatches his other wrist and squeezes the blood and warmth from it. His hand goes numb in a half a second and bookshelf clatters to the floor.

But he's got the deadbolt now.

Paul jerks the door open and shoves her back at the same time, yanking his hand free and charging outside. Carried by his momentum, he grabs the railing and vaults clean over it, landing hard on the blacktop a story below.

His left ankle splays the wrong way and his knees crumple, rolling him naked into the parking lot.

The girl above is a silhouette in front of the nightlight, arms outstretched, talons curling from her fingers.

Then the lamp on the wall flickers out, as if choked by her presence. Her thin form glows in the moonlight now like living porcelain with dark splatter on her mouth, chin, and breasts. Her eyes shine with a predatory hunger: an owl peering down on a mouse.

Paul gets to his feet, limps as fast as he can to the nearest door and pounds with all his strength.

"Wake up!" he yells. "Wake up! For God's sake, help me!"

Then he collapses to the ground again and braces for the next attack.

But she's not there. The stairs and landing are empty.

The door opens.

An old man stands in a tight white t-shirt and boxers, mouth hanging open, shocked at finding a naked young man bleeding on his mat.

IN THE EMERGENCY ROOM, Paul lies in a bed surrounded by pea green curtains. He's wearing a hospital gown. The oversized polo shirt and slacks his neighbor lent him are bloodstained and folded neatly on the chair beside him.

He can hear the stories of the patients on either side of him and wonders if they heard his, what they must think of him: the drunk guy bitten by a crazy bitch he picked up in an alley. He didn't mention the cold or the bestial stuff; no need for them to think he's insane as well as stupid.

A tall doctor and heavy-set nurse come in and out of

Paul's curtained cubicle. He's in that bed for hours getting vials of blood taken out and a pint bag put back in, a tetanus shot, antibiotics, and stitches. Worst of all, the female nurse shoves a Q-tip into the end of his dick to check for venereal disease. The doctor tells him it's unlikely that he needs the series of rabies shots, but it's up to him. Paul declines.

A police detective comes in, a balding man with a thick mustache and reeking of cigarette smoke. He asks for his story twice and eyes Paul like he's full of shit or on drugs. Lab tests say he's not on drugs, but has a blood-alcohol of point-one-three.

"Been drinking tonight, eh?" the detective asks. He lectures Paul on picking up stray girls in alleyways while the nurse wraps a splint around his sprained ankle.

The speech isn't helpful in any way.

"Anyway, I sent a black-and-white to check out your place," the cop explains. "The patrolman found the door open, blood here and there, but no girl. She probably took off to find more of whatever shit she was hopped up on. And took some of your stuff to pay for it. Check your belongings when you get home, see if anything's missing. Let us know."

He leaves his card.

* * *

IT'S mid-afternoon by the time Paul gets discharged from the hospital.

Three different doctors spend two hours debating on whether or not to keep him overnight. Finally they decide to send him home, though he's all for staying.

He'd feel much more comfortable in a big secure building full of people than he would back in his lonely little apartment.

He hangs out for a while, meandering around the cafeteria, the ER waiting room, and the hospital gift shop. Eventually the shop cashier is glaring at him and a security guard comes to stand in the corner. He can't blame them: a weirdo with red, sleepless eyes dressed in oversized, blood-stained clothes with tape and gauze on his neck...

It's probably time for him to go.

———

THE CAB DRIVER almost kicks him out halfway home because he thinks Paul is cussing at him.

"No, no. I'm sorry, sir, I'm calling myself a dumb ass. I shouldn't have been screwing around for so long. I let it get dark outside."

The social worker at the hospital gave him a pass to pay for the cab, since he had no wallet. He and the cabby play tug of war with the ticket; Paul doesn't want to let go, doesn't want to be left alone. But he has to.

The taxi drives off, leaving him in the quiet parking lot below his apartment.

Most of his neighbors' lights are out.

A dog is barking down the block.

Wonder what he's barking at? Paul thinks, then decides he'd rather not find out.

A bloody handprint is smudged on the wall outside his door. Another on the railing. Both are dry, like dark rust stains.

The door's not locked.

Why would it be? I left in somewhat of a hurry.

The joke doesn't ease his nerves at all.

His hands balled into fists, hoping he's ready for anything, Paul pushes open the door...

Darkness.

He strides quickly from room to room, flicking on every light. The cracked bookshelf lies on top of blood stains in the carpet. Brown-crimson crust is dried on the wall nearby. More in the bedroom, on his sheets and pillowcase. The kitchen is undisturbed.

Survey completed, he shuts and locks the door. Paul plucks up the wooden plank and kisses a clean spot on its surface. "God bless this sturdy little hunk of particle board," he says aloud.

Carrying his weapon with him, he attempts to inventory the boxes he'd never counted. None are open that weren't open before. His TV is still here. There appears to be nothing missing.

She wasn't after my things, he tells himself. *She wanted... My blood?*

"Goddamn psycho bitch," he curses aloud. "It was the middle of the night, I was drunk and half asleep and suddenly attacked by a crazy homeless prostitute. All that other shit I thought happened, that was just my mind playing tricks on me. There ain't no such thing as vampires!"

Some soapy water gets most of the blood off the walls and out of the carpets. Scrubbing keeps him busy for almost an hour and removes the reminders. He'll have to wash his borrowed clothes tomorrow, at the laundromat, in the daytime.

Paul settles into his recliner, cradling the bookshelf like a baby. He watches reruns of Andy Griffith, then Jay Leno and late night infomercials, drifting in and out of sleep as they pass.

Finally he digs out a change of sheets, turns out the lights, and goes to bed.

———

SCRATCHING.

At the edge of consciousness, he hears something scratching.

His eyes pop open and sleep quickly retreats from his mind.

He listens...

And there's nothing. Silence.

He rolls over, pulls the quilt tighter against the gauze dressing on his neck.

Scratching.

Something is scratching on a hard surface. A wall? His door?

A jolt of panic catches his breath, turns his body cold: *Is the door locked?*

I locked it, he tells himself. *I know I did.*

Scratching again. By the door.

Paul leaps out of bed, grabs his plank from the floor, and rushes from the bedroom. He's moving so fast that he slams against the front door, his hand checking the knob, the bolt.

Both are secure.

He sighs.

Draws a new breath. Puts his eye to the peephole.

Nothing outside but the railing and the flickering of the nightlight.

Then the light goes out.

The sound comes again, but it's not outside.

It's behind him.

Turning slowly, eyes wide, afraid to breathe.

The closet door eases open. Her laughter from within the gloom, the sound of children at play.

"I waited for you, Paul."

His hands go numb with fear. The shelf slips away.

"I didn't want you to get lonely."

Her glittering eyes flash forward from the darkness. Icy teeth penetrate the other side of his neck. She's rubbing his back and grinding against him erotically while sucking the life from this new wound, body heat drained everywhere their flesh meets.

Paul slips away, cold death embracing him. Lovingly.

MOONDANCE

Even among the sweaty bodies, the overdose of perfume and cologne, and the stink of cigarettes, I can still smell the Irishman's pipe smoke. There is something sweet about it, like orange peel and cinnamon. To be honest, it's a welcome bloom in the wretched bouquet of the Friday night crowd. Out to get drunk at the very least, and lucky if they can manage it. That's why he's come here, no doubt. He knows how to play the odds, and he likes easy sport. And smoking that stupid pipe of his makes him easy prey —for me.

I follow my nose and my instincts. And with the moon nearly full, I'm at the top of my game.

He's at the bar, pawing at a flapper in a flowery headband. Some fashions just won't die, I guess.

That goes for his suit, too. Raincoats and fedoras are all the rage today, not that I'm some department store window clerk. But Red's still sporting duds from the Old Country: dark green, three-piece suit; a bowler cocked on his high-running forehead; and an ornate, serpentine pipe clenched in his teeth. His ginger beard is trimmed neat, at least. Archaic though his look may be, the flapper is going for it. Poor dame ain't got the sense to know a predator when she sees one. Not that he'd hurt the girl, but a guy like him… She might wake up and find her granny's heirlooms are suddenly missing, part of his collection stashed away where hands may never find them.

I slide up on the other side of the girl and grin wolfishly over her shoulder. The Irishman's smile fades out fast, as does some of his rosy color. The flapper doesn't notice, she just keeps talking. I can smell the scotch he's been feeding her.

"Excuse me," I say, holding my private dick badge over her shoulder. She gets a glimpse at it, then eyeballs the Irishman and slinks away.

"What the hell do you want?" he asks venomously. "I'm trying to have a good time, here."

"I noticed," I say, pocketing my credentials. "And you can get right back to stalking divorcées, *after* you give it over."

"Give what over?"

I cock a weary eyebrow. "Come on, Red. The Crone sent me. She knows what you found. And I'm not saying it's fair that she takes it, but fair don't pay the bills, and I work for a living. Besides, you'll find another."

I can tell by the look on his face that he's sizing me up. He's wondering if he could he outrun me.

The answer is, no, he couldn't.

Could he put up a fight? Certainly not. Red's known for his luck, but it ain't that good.

Maybe he can bribe me?

"You know, I've got deep pockets." He flashes me an uneasy grin and produces a shiny gold coin from nowhere. He clinks it hard onto the bar with one stubby finger. "Real deep." A second from the same hand. A third. "How much could the Crone possibly be paying you?"

"Like I said, I work for a living. Can't claim to be a professional if everyone can just buy you off the job."

He opens his hand and spills four more onto the counter. The bartender's taken notice now, as has the big mook standing behind the Irishman. Guy looks like he might be a veteran: shorthair, no neck, chip on his shoulder.

The gleam in Red's eyes turns sly. "What's the date today?" he asks. "Fairly bright out there tonight, eh? But the moon, I fear, she ain't full quite yet…"

He stands backward off his stool, stumbling into the neckless soldier-boy. Swooping the bowler from his brow, Red goes into a little dance and spins the hat in his hand. "Gentlemen! And maybe even some of you ladies. This man is bothering me. The gold on the bar goes to whomever can put a collar on this dog. And double it if he has to limp home!"

With that, the Irishman yanks a fistful of coins from his round little hat and throws them right at me. The soldier's fist quickly follows, and someone kicks my left knee out from under me.

The jovial bar scene erupts into a brawl and the Irishman is well gone by the time it's over.

THE NEXT DAY, I meet the Crone for coffee. The shop she frequents is a classy one, boasting its own superior roast. I must admit, they've got something special brewing in that pot of joe. The smell of it overpowers even the greasy sizzle of bacon in my sensitive snout.

But there's something else in the air here, too, and I can't quite place it...

Selene is seated in the dead center of the place, set up at a circular table barely big enough for two. The Crone, despite her professional moniker, appears to be a young woman in her perpetual twenties. Her luscious black hair curls like an overgrown thorn bush. Her eyes and lips are a powerful shade of violet. And while her black dress covers her pale flesh well, the fit is seductively tight. As fashion goes, she's starting her own trend with that one.

I plop into the opposite chair and she glances up from stirring her coffee. Her lilac perfume slaps me in the face, but that isn't the scent I'm most concerned about. Our table is uniquely adorned with a small porcelain vase. Standing tall from within is a sturdy green stem lined with purple flowers. It was their scent I picked up coming in and it stings my nostrils even more than the pot of java.

"Wolfsbane?" I say. "You shouldn't have."

Her long fingers cross the table and caress my hand. "I knew it was your time of the month, Lawrence, and didn't want you to get cranky. Besides, they match my color palette today."

"How thoughtful." Aside from being poisonous, the flowers also restrict my talents. Now that I'm so close, it's like the pollen is invading my body. I *taste* the stuff and feel like I've been brought low by severe allergies.

"That's a nice shiner you've got there," she goes on. "You look a little worse for wear, today."

"I am a bit sore," I admit. "But I'm still on the job."

She tsks her tongue. "I'm beginning to lose faith in you."

"Don't. I always close the deal, Selene, and I'll close this one. Tonight's the night."

"You sure he's still in town?"

"Why don't you tell me?"

It's part of the dance, a game we're far too old for. I know she keeps her own tabs, maybe even some high-level hocus pocus, but she's not as good as I am. Selene has her specialties, I have mine.

I nod toward a flyer tacked to the café bulletin board. "Street fair tonight, and our boy likes to socialize. He'll be there."

"I hope so, Lawrence," she says, loudly sipping from her cup of joe. "A woman in my profession can ruin a reputation rather easily, even one as good as yours. Speaking of which..." She looks past me. I turn to see a skinny, balding man with his pants hiked up way too far, just coming in. He surveys the place with an anxious, desperate hope in his eyes, crumpling his fedora in sweat hands. "I believe my next appointment has just arrived."

"Hair tonic or love potion?" I grumble.

"Shoo now," she says, waving the backs of her fingers at me. "I'll see you tomorrow, right here, same time. And don't come in with empty paws, Lawrence."

On the way out, I grab her new client's hand, shake the hell out of it, and pretend to recognize him from an insurance seminar. I tell him how good he looks and ask about his wife. He's thoroughly confused but obviously flattered, and I feign shock when he says he's never married. I tell him there'll be lots of costumed nurses and friendly witches on the street tonight, all looking for a sharp-dressed man to have a drink with. "Tonight's your night," I tell him, then walk out.

I hope I've given his confidence a little boost, just enough to ruin the Crone's business for today.

⸺

THE COBBLESTONE LANES are full of people tonight, most of them dressed up. The general theme is short capes and harlequin masks, just fun dress-up stuff, though here and there are costume enthusiasts with more originality. I spy a Little Red Riding Hood showing some leg and it makes me smile.

There are strings of colorful lanterns, junk food vendors lining the barricaded streets, and plenty of beer bottles in-hand. I smell pilsners and ale, beef kabobs, grilled sausage and onions, and three flavors of Macy's most popular perfumes.

This is a stakeout. It may take time, but I'm confident my prey will show up. So I watch from corners for a while, then alternate swimming through the currents, catching tidbits of war stories, ball games, and office gossip. And pickup lines that never work.

I hear someone pitching such a line and detect the familiar smoke of cinnamon and orange rinds.

The Irishman's leaning against the brick face of a local bar. Tonight's suit is a brighter of shade of green than last night. I'm reminded of a movie from a few years back, like he's a maître d' from *The Wizard of Oz*. He's talking to a woman in emerald tights with a feather in her cap; a real beauty and a tall drink of water. Way too tall for him. She's giving him the cold shoulder, but he's choosing to ignore it.

Must not have been completely distracted by her, though. By the time I dart around some laughing party-goers, Red's on the move.

But no way he's faster than me. Not tonight.

So the hunt is on.

It only takes me a block and a half to catch up, and it's easy to tangle his feet without losing my own balance. Red goes down onto the cobblestones. The crowd splashes open like stomping into a shallow puddle, everyone jumping away just enough to let us square away our differences. But it's still thick enough to keep the local flatfoots from getting a good look. I'll have time to work, but not much.

The Irishman rolls over rubbing his arms and complaining of pain. I straddle the little man and grab him by his jade-colored necktie.

"Why can't you just leave me alone?" he moans. "It doesn't belong to her. You call yourself a professional? It's immoral, Larry. You're just a mugger for hire."

I take pause at his words, just for an instant; there may be some truth to what he says, but I've already taken the job.

Besides: "Morality is a discussion for the academics. I'm more concerned with professional ethics. There's a difference," I say, frisking him with my free hand. "But when you really boil it down, Red, I'm just a simple force of nature. The sheep might be off minding its own business, but it still gets eaten when the wolf comes around. And everybody's got to eat."

Hidden in an inside pocket of his sport coat is a tissue carefully folded into a neat little triangle. "This isn't your hanky, is it?"

The worry in his eyes answers for him.

Someone bumps into me from behind. And they smell like they've just rolled out of the gutter.

At first, I assume it's just an accident of the busy street fair. Until a pair of cold hands fumble their way around me, and two more try to grab me by the rain coat. I spin and blindly shove back whoever it is behind me.

The stench of death hits my nose and I start to feel hazy again. Two slack-jawed yokels are too close for comfort. They look like they've stepped right out of a travel brochure, dressed in loud Hawaiians shirts and flowery leis. Must have been a boring trip, though; their eyes stare off into nothingness, their faces are expressionless, and they obviously haven't bathed in a very long time.

No, it's worse than that. Their skin is too pale, eyes too milky to just be drunk, and their stink too horrible for them to still be living. Wherever they're coming from, it was a lot rougher trip than just the Pacific. They're coming from the far side of the River Styx. And yet, they've come prepared. Entwined among the random pansy blossoms around their necks are some familiar, purple flowers: wolfsbane.

"*Selene!*" I shout, shoving one dead man away by the face.

The Irishman slips free and takes off. Three more

dead Hawaiian tourists break from the throng and limp after him.

The streets are too densely packed for him to get far. Red's slippery, but not *that* slippery.

My two dancing partners clumsily try to grapple with me. This being *my time of the month*, as Selene put it, I'm short on patience, and her pulling this stunt has spent all I had. Having two dead guys slap fighting and trying to take a bite out of me would normally send me over the moon, if it weren't for those damn leis.

One grabs my left arm in both hands and bites down, only the sleeve of my trench coat blunting his teeth. The other seems to want brains for dinner, and his mouth comes too close to my face. I punch him in the stomach but it holds like a dried drum. Stumbling backward to escape proves futile with bystanders clamoring around behind me. One complains when beer spills on his new costume, then a few more scream. They must have suddenly noticed the rotten cannibals in their midst.

Changing directions, I surge forward. One corpse trips and goes down, freeing my right hand for punching the other in the head. He lets go and drops to the ground, but won't stay there long.

The partygoers are starting to back away now too, opening an arena for the fight. But kicking and punching only delay the dead.

While one is crawling back up, I slip the lei from over his head and toss it over a girl close by. She's mortified.

I bounce the second zombie into the bystanders and he gets churned away into the movement of the human wall behind him. I've got enough space away from the wolfsbane now, and probably only seconds before some flatfoot shows up.

"Ready to see *my* costume, folks?" I ask the circle of onlookers. They cheer, probably thinking I'm going to strip down and streak the party. Then I show them, and they're all screaming and surging in the opposite direction.

I'm all fur, claws, and teeth in one-point-five seconds. My clothes are restrictive now, especially these damn leather shoes, but I don't have time to undress. One slash of my claws opens the belly of the lei-less zombie. His innards are stuffed with flowers, herbs, and talismans. I yank a handful out into the street and he goes back to sleep, permanently. The other zombie is lost in the tumult of panicking partygoers now, and I'm happy to leave it that way.

I scan the cobblestones for my prize, but there's too much random garbage lying around. Did I drop the tissue, or did the Irishman grab it again before he fled? I could try to find it here, or chase after Red. I'm fairly sure he doesn't have it, so no real reason to go after him. Other than possibly saving his butt. Do I care that much?

I wriggle out of my jacket and shoes, pop a few buttons off my shirt for comfort, and bound after Red's scent on all fours. Navigating the rush of people is easy from behind. I either dodge past them or just knock them aside.

Red has run down an alley and found a brick wall. Three color-clad Hawaiians are doing the braindead two-step, closing on him fast. I leap into the alley and pause— no smell of wolfsbane. That's why these three were holding back, to allow the first two to grab me.

Disassembling them is easy.

The Irishman's cowering like hell now. His feet keep pedaling backward but that wall ain't going anywhere. *Not such a wise guy now,* I want to say, but my jaws can't form words. I growl instead and close on him real slow.

"I don't have it!" he yells, eyes so wide they just might burst. He's got both hands in the air, twinkling his fingers. "You took it! You have it! Please, Lawrence, I don't have it…" His volume crashes into whimpering.

I sniff him good, my wet nose brushing his bristly cheek while his eyes clench behind their lids.

When he opens them, I'm sitting in front of him like the family dog. *Ethics and morals,* I want to say. Everything about this deal has suddenly changed.

<hr>

THE CRONE'S favorite coffee shop isn't as busy the next day. Seems something's got the locals spooked and most of them are staying safe at home today.

A waiter in a green tie brings her something special: a little blue bottle. "On the house, ma'am," he says politely, though she's too busy watching me come in to pay much attention.

"You look surprised to see me, Selene," I say, sitting down.

She blinks away her shock and instead puts on her annoying little tease routine. "Not at all, Lawrence. I was hoping you'd show up. Did you bring my item?"

I hesitate. The silence is more uncomfortable for her than for me.

"You mean your friends from Hawaii didn't bring it back for you last night?" I ask.

"I don't know what you mean."

"You don't?" I growl. "You mean you didn't stuff five bodies with Grandma's secret recipe and send them to cut me off?"

No answer.

"I asked you a question, *Crone.*"

"Don't call me that," she snaps. She fiddles nervously with the blue bottle on the table. "I suppose I did. It was your fault, Lawrence, you're the one who gave me doubts."

"I'm a professional," I tell her. "And that was some very *un*professional double-play you tried to pull over on me."

"Well, did you get it or not?"

I place a folded triangle of tissue on the table and hold it down with a rather pointy fingernail. "Where's the other half of my money?"

She produces a rubber-banded roll of bills from beneath the table. We trade.

"What the hell is this?" she screeches, holding the little green clover between forefinger and thumb. "This only has three leaves! I was told he'd found a four."

"I did," says the waiter behind her. The Irishman pulls up a chair and sits down. "But thanks to you, ma'am, it's lost again. I do have other precious little treasures in my stash, though. Like that." He gestures toward the small blue bottle in front of her.

She snatches it up, her youthful face beginning to show its true age in anger. She examines it savagely and sticks it too close to her eye, peering inside.

Poof! Selene vanishes in a puff of azure smoke, the vapors drawn instantly into the bottle.

I catch it in midair and Red inserts a matching glass stopper into its mouth.

"Genie bottle," he quips. "I thought she'd like it."

An old man stares at us over his newspaper with his mouth agape. I send him back to his obituary readings with a mere look.

"So, who keeps the Crone?" Red asks.

"Your bottle," I say, standing to leave, "she's all yours."

"And what about sharing some of that cash, Larry?"

"Don't press your luck."

EPIDEMIC

I've been reading *Dracula* lately like it's a survival guide. Vamp methods, powers and weaknesses. How they hunt. Of course, vampires today don't have to do much hunting. In the literary classic, the victims don't go begging to have their blood sucked out, leaving them chalk-white and wasted on the side of the road. They aren't that self-destructive. But this thing we have nowadays... I can't help thinking it's our own damn fault.

Addiction is a terrible thing.

I'm in the food court of the Wolf Creek Mall filling up on enough calories to get me through a twelve-hour night shift. And I can't help but notice self-induced suffering all around me. It's the job. Seeing the world through jaded glasses and all that.

There's a woman in the corner munching a chicken sandwich and fries. She can barely lift that soggy bun and breaded bird. Her pale skin is stretched over the bones, eyes sunken, lids are heavy. In any other town, in any other time, you might just think she's a night owl, not used to being awake at this time.

But a glance at my watch reminds me that it's only 6:44 p.m. Everyone's up at this time.

I bet she really is a night owl, though. I might even see her later. Find her after midnight, sprawled across the damp grass in the park. Or passed out from blood loss in the front seat of her car. I trace her face with my eyes, commit it to memory.

I'll see her again. If not tonight, some night soon.

I might sound like an insensitive know-it-all, but I do claim a little bit of authority here. See, I'm the guy that picks up the victims off the side of the road, park benches, bedroom floors. Preserving the spark of life isn't just my job, it's my duty. And these days, it can be a horror movie adventure too.

I take another bite of kabob, heavy on the garlic sauce.

I don't know for sure if the garlic legend is true, but I'm sure as hell giving it a try.

Mediterranean is my cultural region for food, but don't tell my mom that. She thinks you should eat beans, rice, and tortillas with every meal, out of pure loyalty. I tell her if she didn't want me to love Greek food, she shouldn't have named me Zeus.

She didn't, actually. But my middle name's *Jesus*—like, *Hey, Zeus!*—so people call me that. Manuel Jesus Contreras, that's me. Night shift paramedic. And tonight, I'm working alone. My EMT partner, Lou, he's out sick again.

"Out sick." I know the real reason. And that no one is immune to the temptation. Can't help but feel a little bit sore, though. Thanks, Lou, for leaving me on my own all night. Again.

This job was only mildly dangerous before. Now, being out on the streets till dawn by myself... I deserve hazard pay.

Three tables to my left is a gaggle of teenaged girls dressed all in black. Goth-types. The whole goth thing was going out of style a few years ago. Took right off again, though, when this whole sick thing came on. Vamps became popular. The thing that kills you, everyone's doing it. What happened to the good old days when high schoolers had booze parties when their parents were out of town? Now the parents are junkies, too.

Or *pasties*. We call the blood donor junkies "pasties" due to the complexion you develop as an addict.

One of the girls loosens up her studded dog collar to show off her neck marks. The other three get all excited, croon over her and curse with envy.

Sometimes people, especially the young ones, they fake the marks. They think it makes them cool. They stick themselves with a kitchen knife or a hypodermic needle. Even from here, though, I can tell these are the real McCoy. I've seen enough of them to know the difference. You take a girl like that, she can probably bounce back pretty well the first few times she's drained. Eventually, though...

One of the girls spies me watching. She squirms a bit, embarrassed. Then she shushes her friends and side-nods in my direction.

The uniform makes them nervous. My arm patch says paramedic, not police, but they can't tell the difference. The whole mob of them scoop up their shopping bags of black dresses, retro t-shirts, and hair dye, and they get the hell out of my field of vision.

"Be safe!" I shout after them.

Only one looks back. She gives a tiny wave of acknowledgement.

Sure hope I don't see them later tonight.

It's getting late. I need to be on duty by 7:00.

Shovel in some rice (see, Mama, I'm a good Mexican boy), finish my beef and lamb kabob and my tabbouli parsley salad. Clean out the little plastic cup of garlic sauce with my last triangle of pita.

And that sauce is like ninety-percent garlic, too. Grind the cloves with a pestle and mortar, add some olive oil. Pure alchemical goodness.

I grab a large coffee for the road and head out. My turn on the twelve-hour struggle of good versus evil is about to begin.

The October sky is dark blue on-high, bruise-purple on the way down, and as red as a fresh wound at the horizon.

Dusk.

Let the games begin.

As I stride from the mall to my office on wheels, I find three skinny wastoids dancing around the ambulance, trying to find a way inside.

Remember how I said there's too much money in the horror for anyone to end it? Brimstone Pharmaceuticals decided to "help combat the crisis" by developing Universal Red, an emergency blood supplement for treating victims. Uni-Red isn't real blood but it can keep patients from sliding into shock long enough to reach a hospital. I've heard that it actually kills one out of ten people it's given to, but apparently that meets muster for the FDA these days. Most ambulances carry it now. And thanks to Brimstone marketing and the nightly news cycle, everyone knows about it. So every once in a while, you'll find pasties trying to break into an ambulance to get it.

That's why these three ding-bats are circling my rig.

They look like they've been sleeping in the park in those same T-shirts and jeans for a week. One of them, the shortest, he's not nearly as energetic as the other two. He's running low. The brainy one—a tall guy made up with eye shadow—he's found himself a big chunk of asphalt from some corner of the parking lot. He comes trotting up to where his buddies are parked outside my vehicle, holding it victoriously over his head. The last guy, all fashionable in a black vest, he raps his knuckles on my driver's side window, designating the target.

"Hey!" I shout, just a few yards away now. They all jump. Pasties startle easily. "Put that rock down and go about your business, fellas."

Eye Shadow shakes his head defiantly.

His buddy in the black vest starts in with the demands: "We want the Universal Red, man. Give it to us, or else."

"Or else, *what?*" I say.

"Or else we'll bite you, homie," Vest says. His hands do a lot of talking for him; he jabs a finger at me when he says that, then indicates himself and his boys. "We're vampires, *full-on*. We'll drain you dry, man."

I can't help but chuckle. I'm no action hero but these

guys don't scare me. And claiming to be vampires? I don't think so. A real vamp would never chase after Uni-Red. It's not blood. It's barely a substitute for it. That'd be like handing a wine connoisseur a cup of grape juice you just spat in and saying, "Try this, you'll love it."

"Bull," I say. "You ain't no vamps and this ain't no ice cream truck. Go get yourselves some help, gentlemen. Or don't, for all I care, but move along. I got work to do."

It's hard to feel sorry for addicts who threaten to bite you.

The short guy finds a bit of inspiration. He perks up and elbows one of his buds. "Hey, his keys. We just take his keys."

They all grin with yellowing, flat teeth.

But ever since the county started carrying Uni-Red, I started carrying pepper spray.

I whip it out and hit their leader right in the smoky eye with a fat stream. He almost drops the chunk of blacktop on his own head and disappears behind desperate hands, screaming.

Shorty perks up and darts away. Black Vest isn't sure what to do, so I dose him in the face too. They're both still lying on the ground, crying, as I pull away.

On the road now and on the clock.

I'VE DECIDED to go back to the mythical roots. Old world legends. I read *Dracula* while sitting in the rig between calls. As a Hispanic boy raised Catholic, I can tell you this: the whole crucifixes and holy wafers and threat of God's wrath cometh, that stuff doesn't work. There isn't enough faith left in this town to give the holy word any power. I've seen victims wearing crosses that didn't do them a damn bit of good. In fact, I suspect it might be like a secret little sign that they're a willing addict. Dog tags that say, "Here I am, ready for a bite. Take me to Dreamland."

That's what they say. That getting bit is like taking an acid trip while on heroin. That it's euphoria dialed up to eleven. A better high than any drug.

And everyone knows it's bad for them—you're losing blood to the undead, for God's sake!—but they all do it anyway. For generations, the "war on drugs" has been waged with cap guns and half-hearted efforts. Along comes this epidemic and hardly anyone's raising a fuss. Except, ironically, the Church. But the druggies didn't listen to their pastor or priest, so why would the pasties?

And I got another theory.

What makes the world go 'round?

"Blood, sweat, and tears," you might say. "Especially the blood part." But you'd be wrong.

It's money. And holy crap is there a lot of money to be made in this mess. Why do you think they let it go on? Why aren't there special police squads kicking in basement doors and nailing stakes through people's hearts?

Well, one reason is that you can never be sure who's what, I suppose. It wouldn't due to have the police ramming a spike through somebody's chest just to find out they were a goth poser, not the real thing. Or that they were a pastie but weren't actually dead yet. It's not the victims' faults, after all. Mostly, it's not. They are *victims*. But we sure make it easy, don't we? The government doesn't really do much about it. And why is that?

'Cause it's sexy. 'Cause you can't tell people not to get bit. 'Cause it's their goddamn right, right?

But mostly because, if you ask me, there's too much money in it. Medical treatments rack up a high cost. You'd think the insurance companies would complain, but instead they sell vamp policies and add fine print that gets them out of paying for your own dirty habit. You have to invite a vamp into your home, after all. Thus, you negate your policy. Thanks for calling in the claim, though, 'cause now we're raising your premiums.

Commercial vampire repellents don't work, but they sell well. And the churches are filling those pews and their offering plates like we haven't seen since the Pilgrims founded this country. But it doesn't do the addicts much good when half of them just dragged their butts in from the street where they were laying in a puddle of their own blood all night. Maybe they get a flash of Hell and the Devil somewhere in that jolt of deathly ecstasy. A little fear of the God that the vamps aren't afraid of anymore.

But it doesn't last. It's going to take a lot more than that to put a dent in this situation. And no one with real authority is offering making the effort.

Just too much money in it. Too bad you can't spend it when everyone's dead. Or undead.

But don't listen to me. I'm a cynic.

I just work here.

FIRST PART of the night's pretty routine. Slow, actually. Which suits me fine, 'cause I'm running solo, like I said.

There's a false alarm. Somebody calls 911 'cause their "baby" fell off the back of the couch. Turns out to be their dog. "Yeah," the lady says, "he's my baby. Is he okay?"

I ain't a vet, but the dog doesn't look hurt to me.

Later, there's a fender-bender with no serious injuries. One of them insists he go in for x-rays, but I'm pretty sure he's fine. Not my call, though. I just work here. He asks about the costs after I already have him loaded up in the back. "That's between you and your insurance company, sir," I call back from the driver's seat. "They're in charge these days."

I also get a chest-painer—more legit—but we make it to the ER in plenty of time.

It's not until after midnight that things get creepy.

I'm gliding through downtown (no call, just cruising) when I spot a vamp and his victim doing their thing. It's a bus stop bench. Someone's sprawled back with their white arms spread-eagle, head limp to one side. It's hard to tell if it's a man or woman from where I am. Hunched over behind the bench is the vampire. They look like you and me—they used to be like you and me, after all— except they got this aura about them. This supreme confidence that practically glows at night. Not literally; there's no light involved, and they don't sparkle or anything stupid like that. It's more of a *glows like a bride on her wedding day* kind of thing. This one doesn't look all that special. She'd definitely be a disappointment to monster movie fans: blue, sleeveless workout top; grey yoga pants; hair pinned high; blood on her chin. A soccer mom vampire.

I'm unconscious of the fact that I've slowed to a stop and drifted right up next to them; in the wrong lane, no less. Lucky no one was coming the other way. Is it just me trying to do my job or is there some other draw to it, some vamp trance thing that took hold and pulled me over?

She's still cocked over her meal but those intense eyes are staring up at me. The irises are spiderwebs spun in circular windows, nearly all white with bottomless pupils at center. Shining like the beacons of twin lighthouses, drawing the ships toward the shore.

The gentle thump of my tires bumping the curb wakes me out of whatever spell I'm in.

Those white-within-white eyes blink beneath perfectly drawn eyebrows. Her pink tongue snakes out and licks the victim's neck. Real seductive, for my benefit.

I've strung garlic around the ceiling of the rig, big flaky white bulbs on fishing line. The guys make racist cracks about me being a Mexican paramedic with dingle-balls in my low rider. I don't care, though. Might save my life some night. Maybe tonight.

I give one dangling bulb a squeeze, mumble a quick prayer my mom would be proud of, and lower the window just a third of the way down.

"Hey, man," I say, talking to the victim, trying to ignore the blood-sucking housewife attached to his neck. "You need help, sir? I can... I might be able to help you."

The victim stirs enough to tell me to go make babies with myself.

The vamp is amused. She giggles. The sound of wolves tearing each other apart.

It shakes me, but I sniff the pungent garlic bulb in my hand and continue to ignore her. "You don't have to do this, sir. I can get you help."

Notice how I said, *can get you help*? No way I'm getting out of the rig.

"Don't need it!" he cries. "Go away! You're ruining it!"

The vamp hooks the air with one long-nailed finger, offering to let me join the party.

"Can't help you if you don't want help, sir. Just say the word—"

"*Die!*" he screeches, never moving more muscles than required to curse and clench his jaw in anger. A blob of crimson bubbles up from his wound as he does so, breaks and runs down the front of his sweatshirt. "Get lost! Leave me alone!"

Sexy soccer mom shrugs her shoulders, then pats the bench next to him.

That thing about having to be invited, by the way, that's real. Once you go that far, though, it's harder to say no a second time. Harder still the time after that.

I roll up the window, back the rig off the curb, and drive away. That's when I feel my pulse in my throat and realize just how terrified I really was the whole time.

In the side mirror as I pull away, all I can see is the victim, lying in his own blood and ecstasy, slowly killing himself for a quick high. The vamp casts no reflection. That part of the legend is real too. She could be clinging to the side of the ambulance and I wouldn't see her. Until it's too late.

EVENTUALLY, they do all die from it. At some point, be it the first time, second, tenth, whatever, all vampire victims lose too much, go into shock, and die. Or their bodies just give up from the repeated stress, even while there's still juice in the tank. The old mortal coil can only take so much parasitic bliss, I guess.

But they don't all turn into vampires. Just 'cause you're drained to death doesn't mean you'll wake up ready to be the next blood-sucking bliss dealer in the neighborhood. Despite Van Helsing's warning, that part turns out to not be true. Only they know how to make more of their kind. And, lucky for us, they generally hold tight to those franchise rights. Maybe they just don't want the extra competition?

All I know is, people die of blood donor overdose every day. Some junkies probably romanticize it, thinking they're investing in their own immortal futures or forming some special bond with their master vamp, something erotic and unique to them. But in the end, they're all just juice boxes slurped dry and left littering the side of the road. They die for a quick high, nothing more. Only the vamps benefit. And a handful of businessmen and CEOs with the same amount of moral conscience.

———

ABOUT 1 A.M., I get a call. Police are already on the scene. Two adult victims found in their home. And it was a child that dialed 911.

There's just one cruiser outside when I arrive, blue and red lights spinning silently. It's a nice, middle-class neighborhood. A few gawkers stand around on the sidewalks in their PJs and fuzzy slippers. A few more look on from behind the safety of their bedroom windows.

Ophelia must see me pull up on the curb. She comes outside with a little girl walking under her arm, wrapped in a blue and white bedspread. The blanket looks like waves perpetually crashing. The girl's maybe seven or eight with curly blonde hair.

Ophelia Harker is a rough and tumble police officer, probably the toughest person I know. Maybe being the first female African-American on the force made her that way, but I don't think so. I think she's always been tough. And nights like this, they just make her tougher.

I kneel down as they approach and speak to the girl. She looks pretty resilient, too, despite the eyes all puffy from crying.

"Hi. My name's Zeus," I tell her. "What's your name?"

She's afraid to answer at first, but Ophelia assures her that I'm here to help. "Harriet," she says meekly. "My dad calls me Harry." Then she's quick to add, "But my dad's hurt and won't wake up. My mom won't either. Are they going to be okay?"

"That's what I'm here to find out, Harry." I show her the patch on my uniform.

"Are you a doctor?"

"I'm the doctor's assistant. Can I take a look at you, too?"

Harry nods.

"I didn't see a mark on her," Ophelia tells me, "but do your thing, Z."

My findings are the same: Harry's fine. Physically, at least. Vamps tend not to drain little kids. Teens are a different story. Mainly, I think it's because a kid would never survive and they aren't into killing for the sake of a quick bite. They want long-term customers. Plus, they start killing kids, maybe someone would finally stand up and do something about it.

Maybe.

Ophelia guides Harry to her patrol car and helps her into the back seat. "Sit tight," she tells her, tugging the bedspread around her and closing the door. She asks a couple watching from the sidewalk to keep her company and they agree.

"What have we got?" I ask O as we head into the house.

I see her face about to break. Ain't much that gets through that iron-like hide of hers, but this one... Her face crinkles up and she can't respond to my question for a long moment. Tears twinkle at the corner of each eye and, when they finally break and roll down her face, that's like the release valve on the pressure inside. After that, she can talk again, not to mention be a hard-boiled cop again.

"Two inside," she says, wiping with the side of her hand. "Mom and dad. Both dead in their La-Z-Boys. When I arrived on-scene, I thought maybe you could give them both a pint and get them to the hospital, but... Too late."

We get inside and there's no noise, no one else there.

"Paul?" I ask.

She shakes her head. "I'm running solo tonight."

"That makes two of us."

Paul Dini is O's partner. He's been missing a lot of work lately, getting pale, wearing the PD-issue turtleneck under his uniform more often. Sound familiar?

The scene's just like Ophelia said. Male and female victims, mid-thirties, sprawled out for a Netflix binge-session in the family room. Both cold and white as hell, no palpable pulses. Both with multiple sets of marks on their necks and arms. And one set's very fresh. There's some blood on the upholstery of his recliner, a small stain under her head on the couch, but otherwise... Not much to see.

On the floor next to the couch are two liter-sized bags of black market, knock-off Uni-Red. Looks like Mom and Dad were planning on recharging themselves after the fun. But that never happened.

"Stupid f—!" O curses, stopping herself just short of disrespecting the dead.

She toes a brown paper bag tucked away between the recliner and the end table. With my vinyl gloves on, I pinch a corner and dump its contents. There's some IV tubing and a single catheter and needle.

"One," O spits, disgusted. "What were they going to do, share *one* IV?"

"I don't know how, but people do it."

I check both bodies again, just to be sure, for Harriet, but they're definitely dead. "Nothing to be done. At least, not for the them."

"Child services has been notified," Ophelia tells me. "And the V-unit is supposed to be on the way, but all their people are on other cases across town. Might take some time."

You'd think the V-unit stands for *vampire*—and you'd be right—but it didn't come out of homicide, like you'd expect. It was put together by the vice squad, that's where the *V* originated. 'Cause vamps sucking people dry is considered a vice, not murder. That's how messed up all this is.

"Let me show you something else," O says. She turns on her heel and heads for the kitchen. I follow.

A corner cupboard above the microwave is cocked open just a bit. O opens it wider.

Inside is a collection of orange prescription pill bottles. I count six. Then she sweeps her hand in there and that many spill out, bouncing hard off the counter and onto the floor. Four or five more still hide deeper inside.

"And who's name you think is on these?" she asks, snatching one up, shaking it like a rattle snake and then tossing it to me.

It's an iron supplement, prescribed by... "Doc Vic," I say aloud, unsurprised.

"Yeah," she growls. "Doc Vic."

Victor Moony, MD. He runs a private practice, biggest one in town. Mostly it's a revolving door anemia and pain management clinic. Customers in and out all day. And night.

We in the public services refer to him as *Doc Vic*, as in *Victim*, and sometimes as Doctor Blood. If anyone's getting rich off the whole vampire epidemic in this town, it's Victor Moony.

"I bet he's over there right now," Ophelia says, almost at a conspiratorial whisper, were it not for the vehemence in her voice. Her finger repeatedly pokes at the air between us. "I want to go over there."

I shake my head, not trying to talk her out of it, necessarily, but more in already accepting defeat. Everyone knows the bastard is over there, making money hand over fist, enabling this thing, but... It's the same conversation we all have, like, every week. "There's nothing we can do about it, O. What he does isn't illegal."

"It sure as hell ought to be!"

"It's not."

"It is in my book!"

"Your book don't count," I tell her. "No one's reading your book."

I can see that offends her, so I add, "I am, O, you know that. I'm reading it, all us uniforms are. Well, most of us, anyway. But we just work here. They don't read our books." My thumb indicates phantom bureaucrats some-where behind me. "They don't give a damn about us, or them."

"Well, I do," she declares, eyes wide. "I do, Zeus. I give a damn."

"I know you do."

We both hang out for the V-unit and the counsellor from child services. He keeps Harry and the neighbors distracted while I help bag her parents and wheel them out to the coroner's van. Eventually, the mess is semi-cleaned up and the crowds disperse. Leaving just me and Ophelia behind.

She comes striding out of the house like she's got somewhere to go. She moves with a purpose around the hood of her cruiser toward the driver's seat. "Alright, Zeus. You don't have a partner and I don't have a partner. I say we stick together. We'll probably get called to the same shit show anyway, right?"

"Yeah, okay. Makes sense to me," I agree.

"Good." The word has weight. Like I just agreed to something serious. "Follow me."

She ducks into her car and slams the door. I climb

aboard my rig, a little bit anxious. I think I know where we're headed.

"THE CASTLE," they call it. It's a strip mall with brick veneer and these stylish little parapets on the corners. There's a Dollar Store in there, a Chinese takeout place, one of those sketchy check-cashing joints, and the office of Doctor Victor Moony and Associates.

It's those associates that I'm worried about.

And even though it's almost 4 a.m. and dark as hell, there's a line of people waiting at the door.

My ambulance follows Ophelia's cruiser into the parking lot. We glide in slow and silent, but not unnoticed. A few people cut out of that line and either step lively to their cars or fade away into the shadows. One of them drops something that two others briefly fight over, before resuming their places. The presence of a police car has definitely added a nervous dance and tick to those left waiting, but they still refuse to be deterred.

"I knew it," O growls. We've swung around so our driver's side windows align.

"A few of them had sense enough to leave," I remark. "Or shame enough."

Ophelia shakes her head. "I don't even care about them—the junkies, the pasties. They're stupid, but stupid ain't a crime. Them bastards preying on them..."

"The doctor's in," I quip. Maybe humor isn't quite appropriate in times like this, but it's my only defense. Just in case the garlic dingle balls don't work.

"And so are his buddies, no doubt."

"Then what's our next move?" I can see the answer in O's eyes, so I try to talk her out of it before she can respond. "We scared some home, right? See and be seen, police presence and all that? Maybe saved some lives there."

"Until tomorrow night." Her voice is steady, her glare unwavering. "Or the night after that. And these guys..." She nods toward the line awaiting their beloved executioners. "You think I can just drive on knowing what they're up to?"

Just then, the police radio squawks at her. It starts to report an actual crime in progress, a sanctioned need for police support, but O switches it off.

I feel that hard click and absence of audio static in my chest. I know right then that we're going in and there's no way I can talk her out of it. And I sure as hell can't let her go in alone.

I draw a deep breath, sigh, and mentally sign on for this ride. I'm all in now; I have to be.

"I've been reading *Dracula* lately," I tell her, taking down my papery white dingle balls. The strings were designed from the beginning to easily loop into necklaces. I hand one down through my window, which she takes with confusion. When I lasso another around my head, she gets it.

"You can't be serious, Zeus." She sticks her nose to a bulb. "How long these been hanging in there? They stink. I ain't wearing this."

"O..."

"This is silly."

"What about this *ain't* silly? Better safe than sorry, right? You don't expect to get into a shoot-out, but you still put on your vest every shift, right?"

Reluctantly, she loops it over her head. "I feel ridiculous." Now her face shows that sense of *silly* loud and clear. Maybe too silly to continue? For a second, I think I've just gotten us out of a showdown with the undead.

Then her door opens, she steps outside, and slams it closed. With her standing now, we're a lot closer to face-to-face. "You coming, *partner*?"

"All in," I mumble aloud.

First, I retrieve my secret weapon from between the cab seats, then I join her on the asphalt. And she arches that eyebrow again.

"My *abuela's* good dinnerware," I explain. "Fourteen inches of genuine silver-plated, column-style candlestick. Don't tell my mom."

The thing is like a mace in my hands. And it still carries a hint of the cinnamon-spice candle that sat atop it. Or is that just my imagination? I pat the bulky business end of my weapon against my open palm. "It's like in that game, *Clue*. Doctor Blood, in the office, with the candlestick. Game over."

Ophelia rolls her eyes and pulls the nightstick from her belt. "Mine's bigger than yours." Then she pats the taser and 9mm on either hip. "You think I need silver bullets, Z? Aren't those for killing werewolves or something?"

"Honestly, Ophelia, I hope we aren't shooting anybody here tonight."

"Me too," she says, not very convincingly. "Let's go."

I follow in her wake as O strides up to the brick storefront. The door and big lobby window feature heavily frosted glass, to the point of being almost opaque. There's a faint grey glow inside, like dusk in a black-and-white horror movie. I notice the posted hours: 10 a.m. to 4 p.m., M-F. These customers must be on the preferred client list. Or the doctor just doesn't advertise primetime care. I didn't think Doc Vic would actually be hosting vamp night. I figured he was just profiting from the residuals. *Residuals* meaning treatments. If there's a real vamp inside, then he's actually taking part in *causing* the disease that he then charges people to treat. In that case, the system's more messed up than I thought.

"So much for the Hippocratic oath," I mumble. O doesn't hear me. She's in crowd control mode.

Bam! She starts by rapping her nightstick against the glass. If a cop marching up to the junkie line in the middle of the night didn't get their attention, that sure did.

"This office is closed!" Officer Harker declares.

Half a dozen pasties wait impatiently for their turn...

Then two of them peel away and take off.

"You can't do that!" one stubborn customer complains. He's tall and skeletal. That blue flannel shirt looks like it's hanging in a closet on his wasted frame.

"The hell I can't," O growls, leveling the stick toward his face.

The line leader ducks under the baton and dashes off. A paper ticket chases after him on the night air. The flannel shirt snatches at it desperately in a sudden movement that triggers Officer Harker into action.

She's got the guy flipped over and pinned on the blacktop in a blink.

Another pastie bows out. The last one's crouched and

ready, like a wild animal. He hasn't decided what to do yet, fight or flight.

I instinctively mimic him: knees bent, arms up, silver-plated mace ready for action. My heart's pounding so hard I can hear it in my ears.

"Zeus, if that guy's still standing there in three seconds," O shouts, one knee on the flannel's chest and the nightstick up under his chin, "shoot him."

The wild animal and I lock eyes. Both of us are scared, I have no doubt.

But the pastie buys O's bluff. He takes off.

Big sigh of relief. I almost admit to nearly peeing my pants, but I don't want to shake Ophelia's confidence in her partner. Funny how I didn't sweat those three losers just six hours ago, and I was alone at that time. Then again, the sun was still technically up. And I hadn't yet come face to face with a real vamp. And I wasn't standing outside Doc Vic's all-night blood donation clinic.

"What the hell are these?" she demands of her prisoner. The paper tickets have numbers on them, just like we're at a deli or pharmacy.

"Lottery," the tall pastie groans.

"Makes sense," I say. "I guess even a vampire can only drink so much in one night."

"Makes me wonder how many are inside, though." Ophelia shifts more of her weight onto the man's sternum. "You got an answer for that?"

"I ain't telling you nothing!" he wheezes.

Flannel regrets that, if the cry of pain is any indication.

Right at that moment, I imagine another police car

pulling up and us having to explain what the hell is going on. I wouldn't feel relief, just caught doing wrong.

But that doesn't happen. O and I are on our own. No one else wants to mess with Doc Vic. He's like the mayor in this town, but with a higher approval rating.

"How much?" she demands. Her off hand does a quick pat-down of his pockets and waistband. She doesn't turn up any weapons, wallet, anything. "How much they charge to bite your neck and suck the life out of you?"

"*Nothing*," he hisses. "Bliss is free. The ride is free. Everlasting life, all *free!*"

O glances over her shoulder at me. We share a look of horror and understanding.

Cheaper than pain pills, cheaper than heroin. No wonder it's so easy to get them hooked.

And the shady clinics, the pharmaceutical companies, the Medicare scammers, they all make money on the treatments. It's practically free for them, too. Pure profit.

"Get up!" O drags the guy to his feet, slams him once against the brick storefront, then flings him toward the night. He stumbles into the parking lot and nearly falls on his face again. "Get the hell out of here. Go home. Or I'll run you in."

He goes, but not willingly. About halfway to the street, he crouches down and sits on the blacktop. Silent protest. But far enough away not to be a threat anymore.

Now it's just me and my partner. And whoever might be inside.

"Stay behind me," Ophelia instructs me, ready to breach Victor Moony's house of horrors with her 9mm in both hands.

I make a couple of practice swings and defensive blocks with my dinner mace, tug on my own necklace string to ensure it's still there, then give her a nervous nod.

O leads with the gun.

The glass door isn't locked.

Inside, the lobby is empty. It's in black and white, too, like an old creep-fest movie. Grey-upholstered chairs and couch; a black magazine rack; a flat-screen TV switched off; a painting of zebras drinking obliviously from a stream while a lion stalks in among the brush. The receptionist window is a counter protected by more frosted glass. The lights are low, half the fluorescents lifeless in ceiling. There's a door cocked open with nothing but darkness beyond it.

I bob my weapon toward the door and whisper, "Looks like an invitation. I don't like it."

"Me neither," O whispers back.

She pulls a small Maglite from her police officer's belt, cross-bars her firing arm with her flashlight arm, and shines it through the smoky glass of the secretary's suite. Much of the searchlight's glow is reflected by the frosting, but there appear to be no silhouettes lurking back there. O gives me a half a breath to object, then moves toward the open door.

It swings wider, coaxed by her foot. Somewhere in my subconscious, I expected it to sound like a coffin creaking open, but the door makes no sound. Her flashlight probes along the walls, all the way to the flower-and-vase still-life hanging at the far end. It's a hall of doors, every one of them closed. Each has a placard posted outside: "Exam Room 1," "Exam Room 2," et cetera.

There's a switch on the wall. I silently ask if I should turn the lights on ('cause that'd sure make *me* feel better!), but she shakes her head. "Maybe they don't know we're here yet," she whispers, so quiet I barely hear her. It's more lip reading than ear work.

We hesitate, pausing. Are we listening for noise or just not sure what to do next?

Then I hear it: Breathing. Heavy breathing. Slight moaning.

It's coming from the door on the left, Exam Room 1.

Ophelia mouths a count of three, I turn the knob, and she barrels in, gun ready.

A dark shape lies limp on the exam table, a heap of clothes and misery. Two figures blunder inside on the mirror above the sink, opposite wall, and I swear I almost crap my pants seeing that motion in my peripheral vision. It's us, of course, but I need another full second to start breathing again.

O pulls me inside, shuts the door, and turns on the light.

The figure on the table groans and rolls away from us, shielding his eyes. He's hidden in a black hoodie and jeans, too tall to fit on there, even in the fetal position. The thin paper drape beneath him has large spatters of blood on it. There's more on the vinyl cushion and a few drops on the white-tiled floor.

"He's alive, at least," I whisper.

"Then he's not our problem," Ophelia says. "Not why we came."

My mouth hangs open for a second, not believing that I have to explain this. "I'm a paramedic, O. This *is* why I'm here. I need to treat him."

"Keep your eyes on the prize, Z. Focus. The scene isn't safe yet."

"Z?" the victim grumbles. He rolls toward us again, barely staying on the table, and I see his face. Pale, ashen, but recognizable.

"*Lou?*" It's my absent partner. The EMT who's usually driving the rig with me, who had called in sick yet again. I shouldn't be so surprised. I've long suspected he was a pastie, just didn't think I'd ever have to see it with my own eyes.

If Lou wasn't so far gone, so deep into the blood-drained bliss, he might have been ashamed. Instead, he cracks a tiny smile. "Hey, buddy. You finally come to join up?"

I grab Lou by the wrist and check his pulse. Its quick and thready. Trying to keep up with demand, but his blood volume is so low, it's just a matter of time before his body gives up.

Ophelia and I lock eyes. She knows what I'm going to say.

"Damn you, Lou," she grumbles, "you piece of dirt."

I want to point out that her own partner is no better, but take her advice instead: I focus on what matters. "He needs a fluid bolus and pint of Uni-Red. I've got three bags in the rig."

She stubbornly shakes her head. "We're busy here."

"It's *Lou!*" I argue, trying not to be loud. "And he's going to die!"

"He made his choice!" she barks.

My face smolders into a scowl and I leave, fling open the exam room door, bolt through the lobby and back into the night without a thought to whatever might be between me and the ambulance.

The rear doors of the rig fly open so hard that they bounce back and hit me in the butt as I'm climbing aboard. The back of the ambulance is stocked with supplies. Some of what I need could very well be in Moony's office, but the cardinal rule is: trust the gear you know, not the gear you don't. I grab what I need—an IV starter set, Y-tubing, a liter of saline, and the precious blood supplement—then kick out a duffle bag to carry it all. The Universal Red is kept in a locker. I wear the key around my neck.

Just as I've got my arms full, something hits me from behind.

The shadow looms up from the open doors a split second before his weight plows into me, but I'm too slow to see it coming. We both get bashed against the forward bulkhead. Then teeth clamp down on my right ear and an animalistic groan is all I can hear.

Instinct kicks in. My arms and legs fire spring-loaded, shoving the bastard away from me. That's when I see it: the baggy, blue flannel shirt.

He trips backwards over the gurney locked to the floor. His skeletal face is all anger and blood—*my blood*—and he whips around like a turtle trying to right itself.

Just as he's rising for battle again, he catches a stream of pepper spray right in the face.

Then I toss the can and leap on top of him. "*Son of a... Bite me!*" I'm grumbling, pounding him into submission with painful knuckles. I'm a healer, not a fighter. Only ever been in a few scrapes in my whole life. But I'm not about to give this creep the chance to come back on us a third time.

After pummeling the pastie nearly unconscious, my ear dripping all over the place, hand aching like hell, I strap the flannel skeleton down to the gurney. Then I dose him again with the pepper spray. Screw him.

He's screaming bloody murder inside the locked ambulance as I hurry back to the office with my duffle-load of medical supplies.

The lobby's still empty, silent, and creepy.

Exam Room 1's door is still ajar.

But Ophelia is nowhere to be seen.

Lou's on the table, no longer moaning. No longer moving.

I pause there for just a second in the eerily quiet dark, listening for any sign of... *anything.* Then I shuffle inside the room and carefully close the door.

"I'm going to set you up," I whisper to Lou, dragging him to the floor, "then go find O. And if anything's happened to her, you selfish ass, I'm blaming you!"

My ear drips as I set up the lines. That's when I notice what isn't hanging around my neck anymore: the garlic. Must have been ripped off in the fight. I'm shaking my head as the needle slides into Lou's flattened-out vein. "No sense worrying about that now. Don't even know if it'd have done any good anyway."

The saline and the Uni-Red start running on gravity power. I've got them set in the sink and am looking around for something higher to hang them from.

That's when the door swings open behind me.

The mirror is right in front of me. My breath catches

in my throat but there's nothing there. Only the growing rectangle of darkened hallway as the door moves. No one's there.

Yet the strength of a bear grabs me from behind and throws me against the wall.

My body cracks the drywall, then clips the edge of the exam table on my way to the floor. The wind's been knocked from my lungs along with all sense from my head. I lie on the cold tile and suck dirt for what feels like a long minute. Then I hear a familiar voice.

"What up, Z? Ophelia drag you in here?"

"Paul?" I groan.

Officer Paul Dini. Ophelia's partner.

"Funny, huh?" Paul scoffs. "It's a damned reunion here tonight. You and O, me and Lou."

My senses start falling in line. A pair of midnight blue Nikes stares at me, even with my face. Above them are Paul's navy blue sweatpants and a police department T-shirt. My head doesn't twist around quite enough to see his face, but maybe that's better. Seeing actual pointed teeth in his mouth right now might shake my nerves too far.

But I smell something down here, too. Garlic...

My gaze shifts to the corner, behind the door. Lying there is the other garlic necklace, the one Ophelia was wearing. Discarded.

"Where is she?" I ask, getting up to all-fours.

"She's fine. Doc's got her in the other room."

I wait on hands and knees. The garlic string is in front of me, in reach if I dare go for it. I don't know what the hell I'll do with it, exactly, but if he got her to ditch it, it must hold some threat, right? What about the silver mace candlestick? Not in my immediate field of vision. But I know it's here. It was in the duffle bag. I unpacked it along with everything else. Didn't I?

"So, Doc Vic is a vamp after all?" I ask, stalling. For whatever good it does me; no miracle plan to save our butts is coming to mind.

Paul waves dismissively. "Nah. He'd like to be. Begged me to make him a 'made man,' you know? But he's worth too much where he is. Why screw up a good thing?"

"Should have figured," I say. "You being on night shifts and all."

Paul belts out a good belly laugh. "You never seen me in the day time, Zeus? C'mon. That's just Hollywood bull. Sunlight don't kill me. Just weaker in the day. And tan too easy."

Feet clatter in the hallway outside. Someone stumbles in front of the exam room door.

It's Ophelia, all out of breath. "How 'bout electricity, you son of a bitch?"

Two tiny darts on wires fire from the hall into Paul's shoulder. I hear the crackle of taser juice arcing into his body.

This is my chance.

I grab the garlic necklace with my left hand, pivot onto one knee, then ram straight into Paul. The taser stings me at just the moment of contact, then Paul slams without me against the opposite wall.

Poor Lou is taking up much of the floor in here. My eyes scan his unconscious form looking for—*the candlestick*, cradled between his legs!

Paul bounces back with supernatural speed. His hand clamps down hard on my neck. Something pops and paper crinkles as my head gets stuffed sideways against the exam table.

He drops me on top of Lou and knocks the taser darts clear with a wave of his hand.

Paul flashes away.

I don't see where. All I do see is Lou's pale face, inching toward death.

I spin around, snatch the candlestick, and force myself to my feet.

Paul's got Ophelia. They're standing in the doorway, her a human shield. O's left eye is blackened and her lower lip is busted open. But I don't see any marks on her throat. Yet.

"Looks like you guys are the lottery winners tonight." Paul smiles over O's shoulder. His upper lip pulls back, showing a row of pointy shark's teeth. There's dry blood crusted in his five o'clock shadow. "Sorry, partner, but you've left me no choice."

O struggles but can't move. She stops when that hot breath hits her neck.

"I've been reading a lot lately," I say. I have to say something to stop his advance. "And eating a lot of *garlic!*"

The string in my left hand whips around in a wide arc, past Ophelia's head, and slaps Paul across the face.

He jerks away like he's been hit by the pepper spray.

Ophelia dives sideways.

I bring the big silver-plated mace around in my right fist. It's an awkward swing, far from perfect, and doubt flashes through my mind, me thinking it won't be enough to hurt him. But the bulky column of candlestick makes contact and the alchemy alone is enough. The blow wipes away a layer of pink flesh, as if the thing were bladed instead of blunt. He staggers backward into the darkened hallway with a meaty slice of cheek shining like raw beef.

He crashes against the opposite door. I'm starting to think we have the advantage. Then his eyes flick back up at us, shining white in the dark. His teeth glisten with slobber against the room's pale light. Paul's showing us what he's become. No longer human but a monster that preys on the weaknesses of others. He's a preternatural animal. And animals are even more dangerous when wounded.

My knuckles go white against the uneven shape of the candlestick. Will it be enough to repel his charge? Or will he just knock it aside and tear my throat out?

BLAM! BLAM! BLAM!

O's backup gun fires and smokes in her two-fisted grip.

Black blood and bullets strike the door behind Paul. He slumps against it and nearly falls over.

By the time my eyes have gone from O's tearful face and trembling hands back to the shadowy hallway, Paul is gone.

"Where's Doc Vic?" I ask. My voice is as shaky as the muzzle of her gun. She still hasn't lowered it.

"Cuffed in a room down the hall. That son of a bitch is going down."

And he does.

PAUL HASN'T SURFACED YET, but I don't think he's dead. I even sleep with a garlic necklace on these days.

And you know what else hangs around my neck?

Ophelia and I both got medals from the mayor herself, awarded at the inauguration of a new addiction treatment facility. It's a big to-do, a beautiful ceremony, and a decisive victory for the good guys. My mom doesn't even mind my swiping *Abuela's* good China when she hears my name over the loudspeakers. And later on the news.

Maybe *I only work here*, but I do good work. And I'm not the only one.

But the epidemic isn't over, and there's new casualties every day.

So let's get to it.

SNAKE EYES

Darkness. Nothing but cramped, jostling darkness.

Bang.

One of the lugs carrying my box drops his end. My head bounces off the wooden interior and some unseen piece of gear slides up and hits my face in a big hurry.

The other guy, the one carrying my feet, cusses at his clumsy friend.

They don't know I'm in here. They don't know the coffin-like crate they're loading onto the truck is not only packed with theatre props and costumes, but also with a real live person.

Live for now, anyway.

If this job goes well—extremely well—I'll still be alive a few hours from now, but the odds are against me.

Traditionally, rolling up double-ones in a game of craps is called "snake eyes." It means you lose. Game over.

Professionally, it's my moniker: Snake Eyes.

I've even gone so far as to have my eyelids tattooed: cute little cubes displaying a single dot on each. When I blink, my "clients" get to see what they've rolled.

And if I roll up on you, you lose.

Game over.

Irony, then. Maybe that's what attracted my current employers into hiring me. Maybe they wanted their revenge to come with a smirk, a little side of humor that sends the Gambler to his grave.

Or, more likely, they figured universal irony was the only way to beat his cosmic cheat, to lever the odds in death's favor. The only way to kill a man who has Lady Luck bound and gagged in his hip pocket.

They call him the Gambler.

The city at large knows him as Marco Romero. He's a self-made millionaire, a big man about town.

Seven years ago, he was a habitual loser.

Then his luck changed. Suddenly he was winning, big. So big that the bad men in charge of such things tried to get rid of him.

But only half-heartedly, really. They didn't see Romero as a threat then, just a cheat. He'd breeze into their casinos, clean up at the tables, and strut home with his pockets full of their cash and a pretty young girl on his arm.

Same story, over and over again.

They figured he was cheating, but no one knew how. And no one would have imagined the truth.

That he was cheating the odds in a cosmic way, a way no one saw coming.

So they didn't see his rise to power coming, either. Pretty soon, the men in charge weren't in charge anymore. Romero had walked away with enough of their money that he started horning in on their influence, too.

Today, Romero owns the game in this town and sits at the head of all tables.

But in less polite company, they still call him "the Gambler."

And, they say, it's time to change his luck.

Time to bring in Snake Eyes.

ME AND MY box get loaded onto a truck. The jerkwads doing the work pay no heed to the "this end up" markings. I can hear them cussing about the weight as they heft me off the dock and fit me in among the rest of their cargo. Set pieces for the opera house, I'd wager.

Then they prop me on my head.

The blood rushes down, along with all my gear. My face gets heavy and brain starts swimming. My neck is wrenched between the floor and the rigid armor vest I'm wearing. There's barely enough room for me to shove my arms out from the cross-the-chest position into performing an upside-down push-up. This gives me a little relief, but not enough. Can't hold this pose forever.

"Screw this," I grumble.

I shift my hips side to side, back and forth. The

motion is small at first, but builds with momentum even in this confined space. The blood flooding my brain shifts along with my hips as the truck takes a corner too fast.

Bang.

Lucky break. My box slides off whatever it's propped against and crashes into the outer wall. Not enough to level me out, but it's way better than standing on my head.

I hope the noise is enough to make the boys nervous. Make them wonder if they just damaged Mr. Romero's precious cargo. That wouldn't do, especially on opening night.

EVENTUALLY, no matter how cold or calculating a man is, someone gets their claws into him. Usually it's a woman. Sometimes it's another man, though. Love ain't picky that way. It doesn't care about tastes, so long as it gets its hook in you one way or another.

Hell, even I've been through it. That was way back, though, and has no bearing on the present. (Or maybe it does. If I'm honest with myself, losing Renee might be why I don't mind shooting dice with Death on as rigged a game as this one.)

Anyway, one of those gold-digging casino girls finally dug deep enough to penetrate Romero's strongest vault. An actress, with big dreams. And she found a man with enough wealth and power to make her dreams come true. The opera house exists because of her.

The Bacchanal Opera House is an extravagant work of architectural decadence. A beautiful monstrosity nestled in among gaudy casinos and towering hotels that just try too hard. It's a gemstone that brings class to this town, a perfect pearl set in costume jewelry.

A reminder to those who hired me that someone took what was theirs and then had the gall to spend it on love and the arts rather than... whatever the hell gangsters waste all their ill-gotten gains on.

Another reason for their jealousy, I suppose.

TONIGHT IS OPENING night at the Bacchanal. Mrs. Romero is playing the lead, of course, while her husband looks on approvingly from the king's balcony. I'm to be delivered to an upstairs prop room. From there I'll find my sniper's nest. Then, to use an old cliché, the final curtain will fall. Either on the Gambler or on myself. The unluckier of us, or possibly the luckier. Chance will play a bigger part in all this than I ever thought possible.

You see, the Gambler built his success on a piece of science fiction. An experimental bit of technology rumored to be on the drawing board at about the same time he somehow ended up with it. Who knows how he got it: stole it, bought it, volunteered to test it?

Really, I bet that's it. He'd have been a great candidate for lab rat on this particular device—the chronic loser. If a gambler of his piss poor quality could turn his luck with a gadget like that, it'd prove the box worked.

Did he off the mad scientist after that? Figured all his troubles were over and decided to keep the miracle machine and just cut all the entanglements that came along with it?

The lucky rabbit's foot, the four-leaf clover, the magic box, it's called a "probability field generator." A cosmic cheat, like I said. It turns mathematicians into raving lunatics. The way a magnetic field pulls metal its own way, this thing twists the odds in its favor. All odds. If anything is possible, this gadget goes so far as to make them *likely*. It's a gold bracelet for Lady Luck, diamond earrings for the Fates; it buys their favor. A dog whistle that brings the three-headed hound Cerberus to heel.

Sounds far-fetched, eh? Not likely, or even possible? Then again, "not likely" gets twisted onto its head by this sort of thing, so it might just be true.

If it is for real, how the hell do I beat it? How do I kill a man with Lady Luck and all the invisible forces of the universe wrapped around him like a protective black hole?

Well, that's the craziest part.

Like I said, may the luckier man win.

***

I AM DELIVERED—JUST a bit worse for wear—to the opera house. The coffin-like container I'm hiding in, along with the other set pieces and equipment in the shipment, aren't intended for tonight's performance. Instead, they're donations from mysterious parties with a professed love of the arts, articles to be used for the opera house's next big show, *Pagliacci*. That's the one with the sad, jealous clown who kills his wife on stage.

So, when in Rome, right? All the world's a stage and all that? On a crazy caper like this one, why not dress the part? Why not go with a flair for the dramatic?

I'm decked out in the white ruffles, conical hat, and frowny face paint of the tragic clown. A phantom to haunt this monstrous opera house. The whole look is hindered by my armored vest, shoulder-slung rifle, and other various instruments of death, but what the hell? It's the thought that counts.

After I'm unloaded from the truck and set none-too-gently onto a floor somewhere, I allow some time to pass. Which isn't easy, as I've already been buried alive in this box for hours now. But I listen for a while and, once I'm convinced the place is empty, I open up.

The room is dimly lit by hallway light shining in beneath the door. And other than me and my fellow crates, it's pretty much empty. An attic of secrets. I shove a wedge under the door to keep out the uninvited, then flip on the lights and gear up.

Another waiting game follows. This job has more down time than most. And more risk. Much more. But the payoff will be good. If I get to it.

Finally: cue the music. It's extra loud from the back-side of the stage. Thunderous applause joins in. Tonight's show has begun.

The Bacchanal's opening play is *Tristan and Isolde*. A tragic love story. Ironically, it includes travel from afar aboard a cramped ship and drinking some poison. Although, in the play, the poison turns out to be a love potion.

I eyeball the vial in my possession. It's a small glass tube, almost as long as my finger, filled with a slick, clear fluid. This is definitely not a love potion. If it were in a heart-shaped bottle, of course, I might wonder.

Take a deep breath.

Pop the rubber stopper.

Take a whiff. Smells faintly of vanilla and freshly cut grass.

It would taste like it too, if the mower were leaking fuel all over the yard. I choke it down in a single gulp, trying to avoid my tongue, but I taste it all the same. No escaping it. The nasty shit seems to crawl back up my throat, even, like it's trying to give me a second chance to reconsider this course of action. But it's too late.

No turning back now.

<hr>

WITH MY RIFLE across my back, sidearm holstered on the right, grapple gun on the left, and chest-mounted surprises primed for use, it's time for my big scene.

I stick to the shadows, creeping along backstage. No one's looking for me. Their attention is elsewhere, focused either on the actors, studying their scripts, or pulling that lever, cutting those lights.

One schmuck is singing the same opening line over and over under his breath when his eyes happen onto the scary clown. I'm pretty deep in the shadows and doubt he can make much out of me. Still, instinct makes me freeze for half a second. Then I smile, wave with twinkling fingers, and give him a wink. The armor-plated harlequin of ancient Rome, or wherever the hell we're supposed to be right now. His face wrinkles up with confusion and a wee bit of disgust, and he goes about his business again, breathing out that line at five percent volume.

Two steps from there and I'm on the ladder, then up on the catwalk.

That grass-flavored battery acid surges in my throat again and reminds me that I'm now on a very strict timetable.

The narrow plank I'm walking sways slightly with each step. Lines connect it to the rafters above me and to miniature spotlights below me. Further down are the actors, dancing about and singing with everything they've got. I hear a strong female voice but don't bother to look down. I assume that's Mrs. Romero, but the venom at the back of my throat doesn't give a damn who's down there. I have more important things to do.

Nearly to the end of the suspended platform, I find the perfect spot. I can just see over the main curtain to the eastern wall of the theatre. Several tuxedos are seated there, one a somewhat chunky man with a white goatee and a proud smile on his face. Poor idiot. What a night for love.

And hate. Ironically, two more men seated very near him are also recognizable. A pair of the very fat cats who hired me for this job. I guess they wanted good seats for both shows.

And that's good for me. One of them must be standing by with my antidote. So when I successfully close this deal, he can save my ass before said deal—and I —expire.

Left knee down, right knee up. Prop my firing elbow there. Rest the rifle on the rail.

I put the Gambler right in the sweet spot of my crosshairs.

And I don't see any magic belt. No shimmer of force field, no lucky rabbit's foot chained around his neck. No reason that squeezing this trigger shouldn't blow his sternum all over the white dress and pearls of the pretty lady behind him.

So, I squeeze.

But nothing happens.

I try harder, but the gun refuses to go off.

So I jerk it this time, harder still.

Bang.

The damn thing jumps—didn't think I'd jerked it *that* hard.

By the time I swing it back and get my eye to the scope again, I find that the Gambler is startled but unharmed. The asshole mafioso sitting next to him, however, grits his teeth and claws his chair arm for a moment longer before that bullet wound to the chest takes his life.

The balcony-goers stand and scream. The rest of the theatre hasn't gotten the gist of things yet, but they're about to.

Bang.

Another miss. I'm a bit spooked now, I admit, but I've never missed twice. This time it's the woman in pearls—I clipped her bare shoulder. She's thrown back into her seat, where she bleeds and wails with her opposite hand slapped over the wound.

I stand up now. Romero's eye catches the movement. He looks right at me.

I pull the trigger.

Click.

Jam.

"Holy shit," I mutter. "It's real."

The rifle tumbles away, falling thirty feet and

smashing onto the stage. More screams, but I don't think it landed on anyone. I'm too busy to notice.

My hands go to my hips. One pulls the sidearm, a .357 automatic, the other my grapple gun.

The talon launches with the pop and hiss of compressed gas, jets across the gulf of empty air, and finds purchase on the other side. I click the line onto the D-ring of my vest and jump for it.

Midair, I'm swinging down, dipping below the horizon of my firing line, right index finger firing one round after another. *Blam. Blam. Blam.* My other mafia employer explodes in a burst of red. The other shots hit nothing. All the while, the penguin in tails and a white goatee—the Gambler—just stares on defiantly. His left hand clutches at something beneath his tux jacket: the magic box, no doubt. The probability whachamacallit.

The arc of my grapple line bottoms out and I'm on the up-swing, climbing in altitude now and getting closer to Romero. After a heartbeat to aim on this new bearing, my hand twitches to deliver more death. But somehow my thumb gets confused with my trigger finger and I accidentally drop the magazine. My thumb hits the release, freeing the clip full of lead rounds to freefall down toward the panicked theatre-goers below. Then my damn trigger finger finds itself again. The shot in the chamber goes high, followed by *click-click*.

I swing right up to the balcony, so stunned by my incredibly bad luck that I almost miss the moment needed to dismount. Then that missed moment gets suddenly more desperate: the grapple talon breaks free and the line goes slack.

I drop my now useless weapon and snatch at the

brass rail, scrambling for it with both hands like a cat shoved off the edge of a bath tub.

I grab it, but just barely. For several quick heartbeats, I'm stuck there, clinging to the wrong side of that rail twenty feet above the floor. And Romero is just looking at me. Everyone around and behind him is running and screaming their damned heads off, but he isn't moving. In fact, I'm more spooked than he is right now, and he knows it. All he has to do is step forward and peel my fingers free, or punch me in the face, and I'll drop into the cheap seats. If the fall doesn't kill me, the poison soon will.

But he doesn't do that. Instead, he offers a little smirk. He eyes me up and down as I hang on for dear life, then cups the air, inviting me to climb up. If I can make the climb, it seems, he's willing to let me keep trying. Maybe he honestly believes himself invulnerable. I almost believe it too.

Pulling myself up isn't that hard, though the armored vest and its chest-mounted surprises do make for a tougher climb. They catch on the rail and I'm afraid they'll go off as I roll over the edge and onto the floor.

Romero claps for me.

"A clown to make me laugh this evening?" he asks. "On my wife's opening night, *no less?*"

The question becomes a roar at the end, followed through with a stiff kick to my ribs. With the armor, I barely feel it. Then he tries again and I grab the back of his leg. He's hopping there as I'm trying to get up. From a distance, it probably does look like some poor clown act.

His foot slips away from me and he pitches forward with a strong punch to my face.

That one, I feel.

"Who sent you?" he growls, fists balled up and ready for the next round.

"That one," I say, still on my ass, pointing to the dead guy in the next chair. "And that other one over there."

When he turns to see the conspiratory corpses, I jump.

It's time for my last move. The box is real. No sense in trying anything else. Time to play my last card, the ace up my sleeve. My cheat. My death card.

Romero spares only a second to glance at the dead mobster behind him, but by the time he's turned back to me, I'm wrapping him in a bear hug. Our faces are so close we could kiss. Time for my surprise.

I spare only an instant to reflect on what a stupid gamble this is, how crazy the logic, and then I detonate before his witch charm can sabotage me further.

The mines on my chest explode. Six little tarts of fire, plastique, and shrapnel.

WAKING in a hospital is a total surprise for me. I didn't expect to wake up at all.

Everything is a sterile shade of white. There are features, ceiling tiles and bed rails, a transparent sack hanging from an iron pole, but it all comes off as white to me. I hear a noise, a fine, continuous tone ringing in my ears, but nothing else. My face stings. My chest hurts. But I'm not dead.

I'm not dead.

The poison should have killed me. If the miniature

mines didn't do it, the poison should have. Unless my nonsensical theory made sense. Unless my insane calculations beat the odds.

My gamble was this: That the machine bends the rules but can't break them. If something is a sure thing, the machine can't un-sure it. It has to happen somehow.

Six anti-personnel mines exploding in a burst of point-blank shrapnel, bear hugged against the man who supposedly couldn't die. And if that wasn't enough, I had taken the poison. I was going to die. I was the sure thing. Chance of death: one hundred percent. So even if the magic box wanted to bend the rules so that Romero wasn't the one to die in that situation, it couldn't. Had I left one percent wiggle room for it to deflect, it might have decided, *Well, someone has to die, so I say it's the asshole known as Snake Eyes.* But Snake Eyes had already rolled his double ones. He was already dead. Even if the mines hadn't gone off at all, the venom was racing around my veins, fatally vandalizing my body from the inside. I was already guaranteed to die from poisoning. A sure thing. A done deal.

Therefore, when the mines went off and offered up another serving of death, there was no one else to deal it to. My hand was already full. No matter how hard it might try to bend the probability, Romero had to take his cards, his share of the odds. He had to die too.

"But the poison," I hear myself mumble. "I'm not dead."

My employers got me out. That was the deal. They must have gotten me out and dosed me with the antidote before the cops could get me.

I had gone all-in ,but snatched back my pile of chips at the last second.

"You're not dead," says a strained voice to my left. "And neither am I."

My head turns, slowly. The tape, gauze, and dried blood on my face resists the movement and something small and wet splits back open as I do so.

Romero lies in the next bed. He looks worse than I feel. I can't see much from here, but he definitely didn't come out unscathed.

"Missed all my vital organs," he tells me. That smirk comes back over his face, though painfully. "You did a number on my guts, though. Tore them up pretty good. Going to need bilateral shoulder surgery, they tell me. But lungs, heart? Still working."

"Lucky bastard," I groan, allowing my head to drop back again.

We both listen to the beeps and hums of hospital equipment for a minute. I run through my head the likelihood of leaping out of the bed to defend myself, should I need to.

Not too goddamned likely.

"Why ain't I dead?" I ask.

"I don't know. I did overhear the nurses a bit, though. Sounded like they found the poison in your bloodstream and treated it. Sounds like your kidneys took a beating, but... Here you are. Might also be that, when you wrapped me up, you got inside the field. It might have changed your luck, too."

"And how is it that I've come to share a room with you?"

"At my request," he says. "I have some pull here. I own the place."

"High roller," I mumble, not sure what else to say. An odd situation, to say the least, and I'm not sure what to make of it.

That's when Mrs. Romero comes in. Her heels click across the tile. She passes by my bed, a tall, thin blonde in a red dress. Had to miss in the stark white haze. She pauses when she finds me awake.

"Oh, thank God you made it," she says, rushing over and taking my hand. She drops it pretty fast, though, probably thinking the expression on my face is a sign of physical pain.

Mrs. slides over to Mr. and plants a kiss on his cheek. "This is the man who saved your life?" she asks.

"It is," Romero says.

It must be the drugs. Or the last few tendrils of venom in my veins. This makes no sense at all.

"In fact, I was just about to offer the man a job," he says.

"You can't be serious," I grumble.

"I am."

"Why would you do that?"

"You're a resourceful man. I make a habit of stacking the deck, and having you on my side would improve the odds even further in my favor."

Disbelief gets lodged in my throat.

"What would I do?" My field of vision is nothing but white-tiled ceiling. I can't bring myself to look at either of them.

"Bodyguard, mostly."

"Ironic," I say.

"Very. But irony is my business partner and long-time companion. You could also run a few other bad men *out* of business for me. I believe you've taken care of two of them already."

Hmm.

"I believe I have."

"I'd say your luck's turning then, wouldn't you?"

I guess it is, but I don't answer.

<hr>

I'M BOUND to wake up dead one day. Of course, that's silly, thinking he'd take me peacefully in my sleep. More likely, two in the back of the head, fully awake. Or one in each eye, where I can see them coming. Holes punched in the little dots of my tattoos. But if the Gambler is willing to give old Snake Eyes another roll of the dice, who am I to argue?

WHAT'S NEXT?

Thanks for reading! The newest book from J. D. Brink is being written *right now*.

In the meantime, please take a moment to:

- Share your opinion
- Join our community
- Read the sneak peek

YOUR OPINION MATTERS!
Did you like this book?
Did you hate this book?
Tell the world!
With a zillion books out there, it's hard to know which ones are worth your time and money as a reader.

Your stars and/or reviews matter! Click here or visit your retailer to share what you thought with your fellow readers!
Thank you!

JOIN THE CONSPIRACY

Whispered secrets in dark rooms. Strange tales of other worlds. The mysteries of the universe.

And they all know about it... *Except you!*

Fan freebies, monthly updates, special offers, and embarrassing personal stuff.

Become a Conspirator and get free stories at: www.subscribepage.com/jdbrinkconspiracy

FREE SAMPLE

Turn the page for a sneak preview of your next favorite book from J. D. Brink!

SNEAK PEEK: ONE-EYED JACKS

What some more dark urban fantasy and crime noir? Maybe with a little twist of Asian mythology mixed in? Here, for your reading pleasure, is the first chapter of *One-Eyed Jacks.*

"What's it about?" you ask?

The Barbarian Book Club summed it up nicely:

"*A great pulp noir piece involving casinos, gunfights, and a dash of magic reminiscent of* Big Trouble in Little China. *Fun, exciting fiction that reads like my favorite movies from the 80s.*"

Chapter One

"Don't you believe in magic?" the bartender asks me.

On stage, cast in purple light, Marvin the Magician pours milk into a hat. It's a trick as old as he is, maybe older. The audience, at less than half the club's capacity, carry on their own conversations and pay the aged illusionist no mind.

"Smoke and mirrors, Jerry," I tell the big barkeep. "I've been on the other side of those mirrors and there's nothing there."

"That's a depressing attitude," Jerry says.

I agree.

"You want a drink?"

"Better not," I say.

The Speakeasy is aptly named. It's got the look and feel of the 1930s, the walls, woodwork, and even the furniture showing fifty-odd years of stains and neglect. Stained glass chandeliers hanging from the vaulted ceiling, dim light filtered yellow and blue. Tonight there are less than twenty patrons in all, mostly couples, and they don't seem to give a shit about the entertainment and his worn-out routine.

Marvin the Magician chuckles to himself, trying to stir some interest. His costume's reminiscent of Vaudeville: a black tux that's loose on his bony frame, a silken cape, and top hat. At his throat is a string tie wound around an old brooch of blue stone, shaped like a beetle.

That scarab is even older than Marvin, by millennia, and it's the reason Edgar and I are here.

Edgar returns from the toilet, wiping his wet hands on his Bermuda shorts. His neck cranes toward a young lady laughing with her boyfriend at one of the tables as he plops down on the stool next to me, fire-colored Hawaiian shirt glowing in the gloom of this place.

Eddie is the self-described "Mexican Tom Selleck," a devotee of the *Magnum, P. I.* television show. But the only thing he and Magnum have in common are the wardrobe and lip hair.

"Yeah, I'd like to make her laugh like that," he says. "Sad thing is, she'd be laughing at *me*, you know?"

He gives me his goofy grin, then sticks his chin toward the stage. "That what you used to do, Jack? Pour milk into hats, hammer expensive watches? That'd be a good way to lift them, right? Smash a Rolex from some volunteer and give him back a fake. Felix probably has a few you could use."

I nod dismissively.

Marvin's venturing into the audience now, trying to stir some participation. He asks a red-haired woman in a scarlet dress to draw a card. She rudely tries to ignore him, but her date shrugs and tells her to go ahead.

"And fortune telling too, right, Jack?" Edgar puts two fingers to his temple in a bad Johnny Carson Carnac impression. "*Nnnnn*, a priest, a rabbi, and an old magi who makes money disappear..." He rolls his eyes, chuckles to himself, and smooths his mustache with finger and thumb.

"You missed your calling," I tell him.

Marvin's victim draws a king of hearts from his hand. She flashes it around the disinterested room, Marvin covering his eyes with his wrinkly old hand.

"Bam," Edgar says, pointing at me. "What does it mean?"

It's the suicide king. My father.

"A hypocrite," I answer. "And a coward."

I rap my knuckles on the bar, extra hard, to feel the sting in my bones. "You know what, Jerry, why don't you give me that drink after all? Gin and tonic."

"So you really were a magician?" Jerry asks, pouring it out.

I roll the gin around in my mouth, savoring the flavor. Edgar stares at me from the corner of my vision. I ignore him.

"Yeah, kind of. I was the *sorcerer's apprentice*, you might say. Ever hear of Damien Deshanko, in Vegas? Real name was Karl." Jerry just shrugs. I stare at the ice in my glass. "We had a falling out. I tend to fall out a lot... Anyway, I learned enough to know that there is no magic in the world. Everything's just Disney bullshit. There's no great mystery left worth exploring. The only real trick I ever pulled was my own disappearing act."

I follow this with a big jolt from my glass.

"Well, you're in rare form tonight, Jack." Edgar's tone is one I rarely hear from him: quiet and serious.

This life is ending, and the drink knows it. Sorry if it's depressing.

"So, uh, who else you planning to make disappear?" The big bartender looks a little nervous.

"Nothing like that," I assure him. "Marvin agreed to make regular payments and hasn't. We're just here to collect what doesn't belong to him."

Jerry steps away to help another customer, a fat man with a skinny girl on his arm. I eye up the bartender: he's a bull of a man, shoulders like mountains supporting a curly-haired rock of a head, no neck in between. Jerry's big, but not bright. It's obvious that he and Marvin are friends, which makes me wonder if Jerry could be a problem, if push comes to shove.

Then again, I have Edgar. Eddie's more pear-shaped with chubby cheeks crowding his dark mustache. He's a caricature of himself, though that's his greatest asset: he doesn't look dangerous. Jerry's bulk is obvious, but I'll bet on Eddie if things get rough.

Marvin's finishing up his act. The audience doesn't seem to notice. This lack of popularity and his known gambling habits explain why he hasn't had the money to pay for the brooch. These days, he's just the opening act for someone bigger. Tonight that's an up-and-coming comedian trying to get attention from the talent scouts down south. But he's hoping for too much on this side of the river. Hollywood-types don't venture this far north into Rails End.

Marvin bows for some courtesy applause and disappears when the lights wink out. And here I am, only half done with my drink. I set it aside and we get to our feet. Jerry holds out a meaty paw, tells us to wait.

Just as I feared. He's getting a waiter to fill in for him so he can escort us backstage.

We wind between tables and into a narrow hallway in the back, barely wide enough for the chubby comedian to pass by. He smiles at us but gets no response. We've got our game faces on now.

An exit sign glows red at the end of the passage and I make note of it, just in case. Another sign is glued to the dressing room door: Talent Only. I go to knock and feel Jerry behind me, trying to bump by to get in first, so I forgo the polite formalities and head on in.

It's obvious that Marvin is the only regular act here. The sole dressing room is crowded with things found at a stage magician's garage sale: trapdoor tables, trick handcuffs, the Cabinet of Mystery. The talent himself is seated in front of a big mirror, cape draped over his chair, wiping sweat from his brow with his impossibly long handkerchief. His lined face melts when he sees us.

Edgar claps. "Hell of a show, Marvin, hell of a show. But if you don't mind a bit of advice, you need a lovely assistant. You know, a cute little blonde in pink tights and cleavage. All the greats have a lovely assistant."

The old man turns away from our reflections to see us in the flesh. "What are you guys doing here?"

"Wanted to catch your act," I tell him. "See if that scarab was all you said it was."

According to legend, the brooch Marvin bought from Felix is an ancient Egyptian amulet that was used by Akhenaten's priests during the pharaoh's religious reformation. It disappeared from Berlin's Altes Museum years ago and eventually found its way into Felix's collection. I don't know how Marvin found out about it, but he's a believer and had to have it. You'd think an illusionist would know better, but the old guy's obviously a romantic.

"If this is about the money—"

"Of course it's about the money," I say. "And I know where all your money went. A little pony told me you lost it all at the track, Marvin."

"Well, I..." The old magician wipes his brow again, looking at the floor. "I was trying to get enough to just pay Mr. Caterina outright, you see."

"Betting on the long shot, eh Marv?" Edgar pokes a finger into a gilded cage of doves, but the birds want nothing to do with him.

I'm aware that Jerry is still behind me, blocking the closed door, so I sidestep and lean against the Cabinet of Mystery, the kind that makes people disappear. Now Edgar and I are on either side of Marvin and we can both keep an eye on the big barkeep.

"The odds weren't horrible," the old man insists. "Just bad luck, that's all. I'll have Mr. Caterina's money after next weekend. I have another show—"

"Marvin," I say, "you haven't made a payment in five weeks. Felix gave you that trinket on the condition you'd be by every *two*."

"I know but—"

I raise a finger toward him: "I'm not finished."

Jerry's bulk stirs to my left. Edgar notices, too, and he stops playing with the birds.

"Marvin, I don't think you appreciate the break you were given. Felix Caterina doesn't do loans. He buys things, he sells things. You were sold this item on a payment plan, which is a first since I've been working for him."

"And they say the old man has no heart," Edgar puts in with grin. "Must have been the Sacred Brotherhood of Grey-Haired Old Bastards, eh, Marv?"

"I've known Felix a long time," Marvin says. He looks up at me with nervous brown eyes. The old stone brooch is still fixed around his neck, ancient blue against his starched white collar.

"Which is why we're being so nice," I say, rolling open my hand.

Marvin's hands go to his neck but they aren't working to free the item, just cover it up. Sad. I feel like a stepfather demanding a boy's favorite toy.

The other boy steps forward. "Hey, guys, we'll give you the money next week, okay?"

"It's too late for that, Jerry," I say, my eyes still on Marvin.

"I don't want to insist," Jerry says.

"Then don't."

But he doesn't heed my advice. I see the big dark shape come at me from the side, but he's intercepted by my partner. There's the muffled sound of fists impacting clothed bodies, an evacuation of air from lungs, and two knees pounding hard to the floor. I don't have to see the action to know the results. I just ripple my fingers for Marvin.

The old man frowns, unties the stone beetle, and sets it in my hand.

One-Eyed Jacks.

Available in ebook and paperback.
Audiobook coming soon...

SNEAK PEEK: GREEN-EYED MONSTER

Tear the Quantum Barrier asunder with 18 tales of thrilling space opera, exciting sword and sorcery, and astounding superheroic adventure!

Here's a 5-Star review from renown sci-fi blogger Planetary Defense Commander:

"This anthology has a wide variety of stories, and every story kept me interested regardless of genre. I never found myself bored or wanting to skip ahead. There are a couple of superhero stories, a couple of military sci-fi, a couple of sword and sorcery that were a bit like fairy tales, a 1984-style dystopian work, and even a werewolf private eye on the job."

Need we say more?

Oh, we do?

No problem! Here's the first few pages from the international contest finalist *The Thorne Legacy*:

The military police had not gone easy on Corporal Cranston Thorne. He rolled the beer can against his blackened right eye, searching for a spot that was still cold. *Getting warm*, he thought. He popped it open and chugged half of it, grimacing as the carbonation burned his throat, then fished a fresh one from the minifridge and slumped back into the couch. The new can's cold metallic surface was shocking to his swollen eye, but it felt good.

"I'll remember that, Jarvis," he said aloud. He and that traitorous MP Jarvis had shared brews and a couple games of darts just a few weeks back. But last night's incident just proved what Thorne had always said: you can't trust a man on duty to back his friends.

The gladiators on the vid hovered in their gravboots, beating their chests and talking shit behind colorful masks. Thorne took another swig of warm beer and imagined himself as a primetime gladiator. He'd wear blue tights with a plunging waist line (to show off the tattoo on his stomach) and a shiny chrome helmet with a yellow Roman crest bristling down the middle. Weapon of choice... An oversized mallet, maybe. Hell, big-time cornball pit fighting might be the only career track left to him if he ended up with a dishonorable discharge from the Guard.

There were voices outside. Sharp and crisp, like obedient dogs yipping for their master's approval. There had been a rotation of two privates—probably all fresh from boot camp with no qualifications yet to do anything else—posted on his door ever since the MPs had deposited him back home. Whatever pair of lapdogs were out there now, they were obviously kissing someone's ass smartly.

Thorne sighed and his cold aluminum compress fell away from his face.

Not him, he thought. *The old prick should still be out on patrol somewhere.* He knew it would only be a matter of time before the Captain showed up, but he was hoping it would be after tomorrow's court-martial. The base judicial system was moving fast on him this time, but maybe not fast enough. Corporal Thorne scratched his bristly chin and slouched even further down in his seat. His green uniform pants were unbuttoned at the top, the belt undone and hanging open, and he made no effort to close them; Thorne intended to show the Captain a deliberate lack of military discipline. He did, however, tug his white undershirt down over the naked woman tattooed on his belly.

The door of the barracks apartment opened. Two buck privates in immaculate green uniforms stood like statues outside while Captain Thanos Thorne entered between them.

"The boys all get tall and stiff when you come around," Cranston deadpanned, turning his attention back to the colorful gladiators on the vidscreen. "When did you get back?"

The door slid shut behind Captain Thorne, who stormed forward and came to a stop at the younger man's elbow. Thorne glanced up, saw the dark blue of the Spatial Corps uniform and the matching eyes that burned like cold stars, then looked away. The Captain said nothing.

"The silent treatment hasn't worked on me since the seventh grade, Pops."

"Don't 'Pops' me," the Captain growled. "Get on your feet."

Cranston Thorne stubbornly laced his fingers behind his head. His arms bulged and the naked woman's legs peeked out. "This is my place."

The Captain's speed defied his age. He stole the vid control, turned off and flung the controller at the screen in one swing, then stooped down face to face with his son, the deep ravines of his weathered face made deeper by his angry snarl. "And the only reason you're in this rat hole and not the brig is because you're my son. *Now get on your feet!*"

Thorne got up, deliberately slow, matching glares with his father. They were almost mirror images, both built thick and stocky, both with stone jaws and blue eyes. The elder's were dark and intense, the younger's blood-shot and ringed with bruises. The father's hair was slate grey, the son's sandy brown.

"Don't look at me," Captain Thorne spat. "You're addressing a superior officer, stand at attention!"

The corporal became rigid, arms at his sides, staring straight through his father and the wall beyond.

"What the hell is wrong with you?" The Captain side-stepped, his glare focused on the blackening of his son's right eye. "You'll be out this time, I'll see to it."

The corporal was like a statue, showing no sign that being a civilian again would bother him in the least.

Captain Thorne looked him up and down, then kicked aside a lump of laundry on the floor. "*Humpf.* It's appropriate that you're wearing only half a uniform, since you've only ever been half a soldier. We'll see how you like wearing brig orange. *That* will be more appropriate." He snatched a green uniform jacket from the floor. Pinned to the chest were only three service ribbons, not very impressive for five years of service, and on the lapels were corporals' paired chevrons. "Do you even know what kind of an embarrassment you are?" he continued. "My son, the corporal. When someone asks how my son, *the sergeant*, is liking the Planetary Corps, I have to explain that you lost a rank. I have to tell the whole damned story again, and how you drag the Thorne family name through the mud every time you decide to play in it."

Sergeant Cranston Thorne had been busted down not so long ago for conduct unbecoming. Now he'd likely be reduced to a private first class. The Captain was having a harder time with it than he was.

"Six generations of spacefaring military officers..."

Not the Odysseus *lecture again,* Thorne thought. The first two ancestors in that proud line were supposedly of the *Odysseus* subspecies, engineered for space exploration. Even though the characteristic Thorne build hinted at the robust nature of Oddies, Cranston had always assumed that particular claim was dreamed up by his father for pure boasting rights.

The Captain tossed the green jacket to the floor. "And not only are you not an officer, but you're not even in the System Guard Spatial Corps. Six generations of tradition and family honor, and with you the chain's been broken. The Thorne legacy, ruined."

Corporal Thorne maintained his military bearing, posture rigid, eyes locked on some distant horizon. "Lucky number seven," he muttered.

Will Corporal Thorne go from zero to hero? Find out in Green-Eyed Monster!

THE MANY WORLDS OF J.D. BRINK

Discover these and more tales of science fiction, fantasy, mystery, and horror.

HAND OF FATE

High fantasy goes slumming.

1 - Dragon Slayers' Guild

IDENTITY CRISIS UNIVERSE

Superhero adventure for grown-ups.

Identity Crisis Universe series

1 - Hungry Gods

2 - Secret Origins

3 - Deus Ex Machina

4 - Golden Age Heroes

Hero Crisis Superhero Boxed Set

Stand-Alone Novellas & Stories

Invasion

Masks

Secret Identities

Dreams of Flying

Tuesday Afternoon Mayhem

THE THUNDERSTRIKE SAGA

ABOUT THE AUTHOR

J. D. Brink was not a private detective in the 1940s, but he'd liked to have been.

Instead he was born in the 1970s, was a kid at the best time ever to be a kid (the '80s), and went to college in the '90s. Since then he's become a sailor, spy, nurse, and officer in the U.S. Navy, as well as a gravedigger, insurance adjuster, and school teacher.

Today (Halloween, 2019) he and his family have returned to his native Ohio, where there aren't enough cheating husbands, missing persons, practicing witches, or hard-boiled mysteries to keep him occupied.

His fictional adventures take place in the Identity Crisis superhero universe, Endless Dark sci-fi universe, and Thunderstrike Saga fantasy realm, to name a few.

Contact the author and join The Conspiracy for freebies,

updates, secrets, and more by way of these cybernetic whisper modes:

jdbrinkbooks.com
writeme@jdbrinkbooks.com
www.subscribepage.com/jdbrinkconspiracy